The explosion turned the house into a swirling sea of flames

Feeling the heat reach out to scorch him, Bolan took two lunging steps forward. He cleared the top of the stone steps fronting the old building, and went shoulder first down the rest. He landed hard, rolling to the wet sidewalk, and lay facedown in the gutter as the fire raged over him.

The dark, wet Chicago night was illuminated by the gushing flames. Mack Bolan lay in the rain-washed gutter, dazed and a little confused by the sudden turn of events.

From what he'd seen in that basement, it was already up and running. Maybe out of control.

MACK BOLAN ®
The Executioner

DON PENDLETON'S
THE EXECUTIONER®
BLACK DAWN RISING

A GOLD EAGLE BOOK FROM
WORLDWIDE®

TORONTO • NEW YORK • LONDON
AMSTERDAM • PARIS • SYDNEY • HAMBURG
STOCKHOLM • ATHENS • TOKYO • MILAN
MADRID • WARSAW • BUDAPEST • AUCKLAND

First edition July 1999
ISBN 0-373-64247-4

Special thanks and acknowledgment to
Michael Linaker for his contribution to this work.

BLACK DAWN RISING

Printed in U.S.A.

When you see a rattlesnake poised to strike, you do not wait until he has struck before you crush him.

— Franklin D. Roosevelt

Know your enemy and you already have the advantage over him.

—Mack Bolan

THE
MACK BOLAN®
LEGEND

Nothing less than a war could have fashioned the destiny of the man called Mack Bolan. Bolan earned the Executioner title in the jungle hell of Vietnam.

But this soldier also wore another name—Sergeant Mercy. He was so tagged because of the compassion he showed to wounded comrades-in-arms and Vietnamese civilians.

Mack Bolan's second tour of duty ended prematurely when he was given emergency leave to return home and bury his family, victims of the Mob. Then he declared a one-man war against the Mafia.

He confronted the Families head-on from coast to coast, and soon a hope of victory began to appear. But Bolan had broken society's every rule. That same society started gunning for this elusive warrior—to no avail.

So Bolan was offered amnesty to work within the system against terrorism. This time, as an employee of Uncle Sam, Bolan became Colonel John Phoenix. With a command center at Stony Man Farm in Virginia, he and his new allies—Able Team and Phoenix Force—waged relentless war on a new adversary: the KGB.

But when his one true love, April Rose, died at the hands of the Soviet terror machine, Bolan severed all ties with Establishment authority.

Now, after a lengthy lone-wolf struggle and much soul-searching, the Executioner has agreed to enter an "arm's-length" alliance with his government once more, reserving the right to pursue personal missions in his Everlasting War.

PROLOGUE

Las Vegas, Nevada

Leo Corbin was sweating hard despite the air-conditioning inside the hotel lobby, and it had nothing to do with the temperature.

He picked up the telephone, dropped in a coin and punched the number. He was almost praying he wouldn't get an answer.

"Yes?"

Corbin felt his stomach flip. He knew that quiet, controlled voice. The unhurried, perfectly formed sounds that really scared the hell out of him.

"Corbin."

"If you're calling me at this time, we must have a problem."

"Yeah."

"What is it?"

"The deal's off," Corbin said. Carefully now, he tried to convey his message with the use of code words in case someone was listening in. "The merchandise has been expended. It was unexpected, so we weren't ready."

"I see. Did you tidy things up?"

"Yes, as instructed."

"Are you on your own now?"

"Yes."

There was a slight pause.

"Remain where you are, and I'll have someone pick you up. The sooner you return, the quicker we can assess the situation and prepare fresh samples for your demonstration. Give me your location."

After the call was over, Corbin made his way to the hotel bar. He ordered a cool drink and sat by the window so he could watch the street.

He glanced at his watch, realizing he had at least a couple of hours to wait, maybe more. He downed half the drink. Beyond the glass, Las Vegas went about its business, unaware of the tragedy that had been so narrowly avoided.

Corbin emptied his glass. He signaled a waiter and ordered a refill. While he waited, he thought back over the past few hours. It had all seemed so clear and simple then. If Kolbe hadn't decided to play clever, he would still be alive. Instead, he was burned to a crisp inside the car Corbin had torched twenty miles outside the city.

He picked up his second drink the moment it arrived. The liquor was meant to wash away the taste of death, the acrid stench of burning flesh. The problem was it didn't. Nor did the next two. But by that time Corbin didn't care. When he went to the men's room he felt light-headed. Inside, he splashed water on his face, spilling some down his shirt. He looked into the mirror, staring at his own reflection. His skin was red from exposure to the Nevada sun. He'd had to walk more than five miles before picking up a ride, explaining that he needed to get to the city and have someone tow his broken-down car. The grizzled old-timer who had picked him up only nodded in sympathy at Corbin's explanation, making some remark about cars in the old days. He had dropped Corbin at a gas station on the edge of the city, driving off without a word.

Tidying himself up, Corbin made his way back to the bar and resumed his seat. He found he was out of cigarettes, recalling that he had left his pack in the car with Kolbe. He went to the bartender and bought another one, made his way back to his seat and lit a cigarette. The lighter he took from his pocket had been the same one he'd used to ignite the gas-soaked cloth that he'd tossed inside the car. He sucked on the cigarette, drawing the smoke deep into his lungs. He sank back as the nicotine calmed him.

Three drinks and half a pack of cigarettes later, Corbin was still uneasy. He was finding it hard to concentrate on anything but Kolbe's death. Corbin was used to seeing men die, but not the way Kolbe had gone. It hadn't made any difference that he knew what to expect. They had all seen the video-tapes showing the exposure trials on animals and humans. But that had been different. Detached. Distant. They had been able to watch and assess dispassionately.

Today had been something else. Seeing Kolbe die the way he had, Corbin found himself haunted by the image.

"Sorry I took so long."

Corbin glanced up and saw Tarrant standing over him.

"Car's outside," Tarrant said. His tone was light, almost casual.

As they reached the sidewalk Corbin realized that Tarrant was never casual.

He paused as Tarrant opened the rear door of the long black limousine waiting at the curb.

"Let's go," he whispered so only Corbin could hear. His soft words clashed with the hard muzzle of the automatic pistol pressed suddenly into Corbin's ribs. His voice hardened too. "Get in the fucking car. Now."

As Corbin slid across the rear seat, he caught a glimpse of the driver. The man was watching him through the rearview mirror, and Corbin recognized his eyes.

It was Erlich.

Everything collapsed around him, spiraling down a black hole. If Erlich was involved, then he was in deep trouble. He hunched in the far corner of the seat as Tarrant dropped beside him. The door closed with a solid thud and the car rolled away from the curb, pulling into the stream of traffic.

Corbin watched Las Vegas slip away behind him and the desert highway stretch to the distant horizon. It was long, painful minutes of silence.

Finally, Tarrant spoke.

"Plain and simple, Leo," he said. "Where did you leave the car?"

Corbin stared at him for a moment, the question catching him off guard.

"Don't waste my time," Erlich said in heavily accented English.

Corbin was still taking it all in when Tarrant hit him. The first blow tore open his left cheek. The next crushed his lips back into his teeth. Blood swirled inside Corbin's mouth and trickled down his throat. More blows followed, hard and merciless. Tarrant was using the heavy automatic pistol, and he carried out his task with methodical precision. By the time he stopped, Corbin's face was a broken, bloody mask.

"Coming clearer now?" Tarrant asked.

Corbin stared at him through a red haze, then nodded, the pain almost shattering his skull.

"We don't have all day."

With great difficulty Corbin told them where to find the car. The effort exhausted him. He crouched lower into the corner, hoping Tarrant and Erlich would forget he was there.

He didn't remember the car stopping, or the two men getting out. He was only dimly aware of them returning and the car moving off again, bumping over the rough ground until it reached the highway. More than once he drifted into a pain-filled stupor.

He was jerked out of it as rough hands caught hold of his clothing and he was dragged from the car. Corbin slumped to his knees. Someone took hold of his hair and yanked his head back. He cried out in pain, his eyes snapping open as he stared up into Erlich's face. The man's blond hair, framing his tanned face and blue eyes, filled Corbin's world. Erlich looked back at him with total indifference.

"I said we shouldn't have entrusted such an important task to an inferior like you. Maybe next time someone will listen to me."

Corbin knew he was about to die.

"Fuck you, asshole," he yelled defiantly, managing to spit out the words before the cold steel of the knife in Erlich's fist sliced deep into his throat and opened it from ear to ear.

Corbin didn't die instantly. He lay facedown in the dirt, blood streaming from the gaping wound. He found it hard to breathe. He was slowly choking, his body going into spasms, but he did hear the car drive away. Then the world began to shut down around him. His senses drifted, ebbing little by little. He began to feel cold. Then it became very quiet.

1

Chicago

Mack Bolan shot the hardman the instant he saw the raised gun. The 3-round burst from the Beretta chewed into the guy's chest and pushed him off the landing. He toppled down the stairs without uttering a sound, crashing at the bottom in a tangle of broken limbs.

The dead man's partners, with crew cuts and sporting skull and swastika tattoos, brought their weapons into play. But as with their deceased partner, these neo-Nazi thugs were nothing more than expendable frontline troops for Black Dawn. They were more used to backstreet mugging than hot combat.

Bolan didn't cut them any slack. They carried automatic weapons and looked set to use them. His incursion into the local chapter of the Black Dawn organization had been to gain information on their unusual activities. Left alone the Executioner would've been in and out quickly. But circumstances had changed rapidly, presenting him with a life or death situation.

The rattle of automatic fire echoed up the stairwell. Slugs tore at the crumbling plaster, showering

Bolan's black-clad form with pale dust as he dropped into a crouch, returning fire with the Beretta 93-R gripped two-handed. The machine pistol ejected a pair of suppressed tribursts, and the would-be assassins were driven back down the stairs to join their dead comrade.

Descending the stairs, Bolan scanned the hallway below. Nothing moved. He reached bottom and stepped over the three, awkwardly crumpled corpses. Blood spattered the stairs, soaking into the scuffed wood. The Black Dawn thugs had paid a high price for membership in the neo-Nazi organization.

The Executioner picked up one of the dropped weapons. It was a new 9 mm Uzi, a sophisticated weapon to fall into the hands of a neo-Nazi organization. Bolan checked the magazine, plucked a spare from the belt of one of the dead men and slipped it into his pocket.

Crossing the empty room, Bolan checked out the next room, leading off the main hall. According to Brognola's information, this was where the group held its rallies. Here the leaders of Black Dawn made their speeches, filling the air with their reckless calls for cleansing America of the minority groups. They'd stir up mindless intolerance directed against color, religion, politics and any other subject they could rail against. There was a need, according to Black Dawn, to purge America of the bad seed— the impure and the foreign.

Now, the Nazi mentality was raising its blind head again, seeking to gain the support of a blinkered minority, using blood-quickening propaganda that still rang with the echoes of Hitler's Third Reich.

Bolan's foray into the Black Dawn headquarters was in answer to Hal Brognola's request for assistance. Information had been coming in concerning a darker side to the visible machinations of Black Dawn. There was also the suggestion that the group was making some kind of power linkup with its sister group in Germany. The details were sketchy, but the implication hinted at financial and political clout being thrown into the ring. Someone in Germany was putting a lot of muscle behind the Black Dawn organization. Recent attempts by the party to field a member in local elections had failed. Despite a degree of public support for Black Dawn, the political arm had been thrown out, the candidate humiliated in public. Visibly shaken by this defeat, Black Dawn had retreated to lick its wounds, but undercover operatives, watching and listening, picked up murmurings that the Nazis were far from finished.

The possible merging between Germany and the U.S. neo-Nazi groups, with its implications of America being targeted by Black Dawn on both political and civilian fronts, heightened awareness in the security community.

Brognola's contact, who had been feeding him information for a number of weeks, had warned of something serious in the works. That was what brought the Executioner to Chicago, on a chilly, rainy night, to a violent reception at the Black Dawn headquarters.

The floor of the meeting hall was littered with discarded leaflets and lapel badges. At the rear of the raised platform a cloth banner drooped across the grubby wall. The banner's red background supported the black silhouette of a wolf's head with its open mouth showing fangs. On each side of the head were swastikas and the title Black Dawn.

There was nothing here for the Executioner. He turned and retraced his steps across the hall, knowing something in this place had to warrant such a violent reaction to his appearance. Black Dawn's heavy squad had something to hide. They had been too willing to place themselves in the firing line for just an empty building.

Bolan spotted a part-open door, a dim glow of light showing beyond it. Flattening himself against the wall, he toed the door open and found himself staring at steps leading down to the basement. Easing through the door, Bolan paused to check for sound. Nothing. Even so, he descended the steps with caution, the Uzi in the firing position, finger light on the trigger. At the bottom he turned right and surveyed the area.

It was large, much of it cluttered with the accumulated debris of countless years. The far end of the basement was in darkness. The section closest to the steps was illuminated by a harsh fluorescent light, which threw a cold glare over the area. Bolan saw that it resembled a laboratory setup, and his first thoughts were of drugs.

As he edged farther into the basement, he saw some kind of construction on the far side, built against the wall. It looked like a chamber, built from thick, transparent plastic sheets. There was a door on one side, fitted with elaborate seals and a locking device. Next to it were a couple of small, powerful pump units, connected to the chamber by flexible hoses.

Bolan continued on; he needed to get a closer look.

A metal seat was bolted to the floor in the center of the chamber. But what caught his attention was the human figure—male by its clothing, despite the shredded state it was in.

He was held in a sitting position by the leather restraints at his wrists and ankles. There was even a strap around his head, fixing it in a rigid, unmovable position.

For a moment Bolan was motionless, his gaze fixed on the wide-open, pleading eyes of the corpse. The victim was dead, but those staring eyes spoke volumes. They had seen the open doors of Hell, seconds before entering, and the image was burned there for eternity.

Mack Bolan had seen many forms of death during his Everlasting War. Every mile he walked in the hellgrounds was paved with the souls of the dead, the innocent victims of savagery and betrayal. He had become something of an expert at recognizing the aura of suffering that remained with the victims of injustice.

And right now, here in this dusty basement, was another example of civilized man losing sight of his humanity.

The dead man's exposed flesh had lost its natural color. Now it was darker, discolored. His veins were so swollen they strained against the flesh. All of the finger joints bulged, in some cases splitting the skin until they had bled. Over much of the skin surface were weeping sores that had leaked a vile yellow pus over the bare flesh. The victim's tongue hung from his gaping mouth, thick and darkened. Sometime during his final moments the dead man had bitten into his tongue, spilling blood down his chest. Crusted blood also showed around his nostrils and ears.

Tearing his gaze from the corpse, Bolan scanned the area and spotted a discarded coat on a plastic chair. He crossed to the chair, checked the coat pockets and pulled out a slim, much-used wallet. There were a few dollar bills, a couple of crumpled receipts and a credit card. Bolan slipped the wallet into his pocket and finished checking the coat. Nothing else.

A faint electronic buzz suddenly went off.

He looked around, seeking the source of the sound. A flashing red light told him a device had been activated.

Crouching beside it, Bolan saw that it was a timer.

He traced the wires running from the device. They snaked across the basement, vanishing into the dark corners. As he looked around, Bolan saw more of the activated timers. Inside the chamber, just behind the metal seat, Bolan recognized a thermal pack strapped to the rear leg.

How many more had been set throughout the building?

It was no wonder the Black Dawn thugs had tried to eliminate Bolan quickly. They wanted to get away from the building before it went up in flames.

The soldier turned without further thought and sprinted up the steps. He was almost at the top when the devices started to go off, and the basement turned into a swirling sea of flames. He felt the heat reach out to scorch him as he dug in his heels and powered off the top step, throwing himself through the door. He slid across the hallway, feeling the flames burst through the basement door.

Bolan scrambled to his feet, cutting across the hall toward the building's front doors.

Then a fireball erupted from the deserted meeting room, leaping in his direction. Windows shattered, allowing air in to feed the flames. The upper floor became bright with howling waves of fire.

The Uzi in Bolan's hands crackled as he held down the trigger, directing the 9 mm slugs into the lock on the front doors. Wood and metal flew. When the soldier hit the doors at full tilt, his left shoulder slamming against the dead center, they burst open. Aware of the advancing ball of flame, Bolan took two lunging steps forward. He cleared the top of the stone steps fronting the old building, and went shoulder first down the rest. He landed hard, rolling to the wet sidewalk, and lay facedown in the gutter as the fire raged over him.

The dark, wet Chicago night was illuminated by the gushing flames. Mack Bolan lay in the rain-washed gutter, dazed and a little confused by the sudden turn of events. If he made no other progress with this mission before dawn, Bolan was sure of one thing.

From what he'd seen in the basement, it was up and running. Maybe already out of control.

2

Hal Brognola gripped the mug of coffee, turning to cross the quiet office. It was situated down the corridor from the squad room of the Chicago Police Department's district precinct, and was an oasis of calm in the middle of chaos.

"Hell of a night," the big Fed grumbled. "Damn plane had to circle for nearly half an hour before we could land at O'Hare."

Mack Bolan watched Brognola as he paced back and forth. He drained his own coffee mug and placed it on the desk beside him.

"Hal," he said quietly.

Brognola continued to pace.

"Hal," he repeated, this time with considerably more force.

The big Fed stopped, turning to stare at him, then sat down.

"I was supposed to be here for you, Striker."

"You are," Bolan told him.

The Executioner was fully aware of the heavy load Brognola carried. The man from Justice was a master juggler, having to keep any number of operations, briefings and interagency meetings going at the same time. He was a man on the move almost twenty-four hours a day.

Now he was there in Chicago, keeping the local cops at bay, and bringing Bolan up-to-date with the current mission.

The telephone rang. The line had been allocated to Brognola, and both he and Bolan had been waiting for a call from Stony Man Farm. Picking up the receiver, the big Fed spoke gruffly.

"You got anything useful?"

Barbara Price was on the other end of the line. She seemed extremely alert despite the late hour.

"The reports came in on the two dead men found in Nevada. Our suspicions were confirmed. The one who had his throat cut was Leo Corbin. He was known to have been associated with right-wing organizations. Lately, he'd been seen in the company of Asher Kolbe, a member of Black Dawn. He was also the second dead man, the one found in the burnt car. He was identified by dental records."

"Anything else?"

"Yes. The medical report on the autopsy detailed two items. Kolbe was dead before the fire, and small areas of his skin that were protected from the full force of the fire showed some kind of infection residue. The coroner felt that Kolbe could have been suffering from some kind of highly infectious disease. He's going to have another look and try to identify what it was."

"Keep me posted," Brognola said. "Good work. Tell everybody thanks."

"How's our mutual friend?"

"A little dusty. But he'll mend."

"Give him my best," Price said, and meant it.

Brognola hung up. "The lady sends her love."

Bolan nodded.

The big Fed gave him a rundown on Price's report, seeing the interest in Bolan's eyes when he mentioned the coroner's suspicions about a possible disease.

"Same as your body in the basement?"

"Could be," Bolan said. "That fire was meant to destroy that corpse as well as level the building. Whatever Black Dawn has been up to, it's doing its damnedest to cover its tracks."

Someone knocked on the door, and at Brognola's response a tall, round-shouldered man in his thirties walked in. He had a thatch of red hair and the haggard expression of a cop too long in the job.

Ryan Kelly was in charge of the investigation into the Black Dawn fire. His suspicions of Bolan, who was picked up barely conscious by a Chicago PD squad car, had been increased when the black-clad warrior remained silent, insisting on his single phone call. It was only when Brognola had spoken to the cop, explaining Bolan's presence in the city as part of a federal investigation, that Kelly had backed off. Brognola had promised to fly down to Chicago and help square matters for the cop. By the time the big Fed arrived, Kelly and Bolan had already worked out their differences and were treating each other with the mutual respect of professionals.

"Got your ID on that guy in the basement," Kelly said, handing Brognola a file card.

The big Fed scanned the card, his face hardening as he read the information.

"It was Benjamin Meyer," he said.

The cop held up the credit card Bolan had found in the discarded coat.

"This clinched it," he said. "Issued in the name of Meyer, too."

"Thanks, Kelly," Brognola said. "I appreciate your fast turnround."

Bolan had already stood, moving to the coffee-maker. He poured a fresh mug and offered it to the cop. Kelly stood tall enough to face Bolan eye to eye. He acknowledged the silent gesture, taking the mug.

"Thanks, Belasko," he said, using the name Bolan had chosen for this mission. Then he grinned. "If that's your real name."

Bolan returned the smile but didn't respond.

"So, what else can Chicago's finest do for you?"

"Give us what you have on Black Dawn."

"They've been around for a few years off and on, starting out as just another bunch who liked to pretend they're Nazis. They had their meetings. Kept it pretty much in-house. Around eight or nine months ago, things changed. They started getting high profile. Bought time on one of the public-access TV channels and started pushing some really scary propaganda. Next thing we had attacks on ethnic-owned businesses, Black Dawn symbols painted on walls and cars, followed by a spate of beatings. We did some checking. No leads. Plenty of suspicions but nothing we could take to court. The group has a real slick lawyer on their books. The guy has all the answers. Every time we pull in one of the activists, their man is on our backs before the ink's dry on the charge sheet. To date we haven't managed to make a damn thing stick."

"Who is this lawyer?" Bolan asked.

Kelly scribbled on a sheet of paper and handed it to the soldier.

"That mother's details are branded across the inside of my skull. I don't even need to look them up." He threw Bolan a curious glance. "You planning on paying him a visit?"

The Executioner didn't reply; he just drained his coffee.

"I need to get back to my hotel," Bolan finally answered.

"I've a few things to tidy up here," Brognola said.

"Okay, you guys," Kelly stated. "I get the picture."

Bolan took Kelly's hand. "Thanks for the help, Kelly."

"Is this goodbye?" the cop asked, sensing that once Bolan left he wouldn't be coming back.

"I could drop in again. You never know."

"Yeah? Well, next time don't set the city on fire to let me know. A phone call is all I need."

Bolan picked up the small sports bag that held his weapons. "My car still outside?"

Kelly nodded and gave him the directions.

Bolan left the office and made his way down the service stairs to the side entrance. His rental car was exactly where Kelly said it would be. The soldier pulled on a long coat to cover his blacksuit, then dropped the bag on the floor beside him and fired up the engine. He eased away from the building, rolling out onto the deserted street. It was almost 6:00 a.m., and it was still drizzling. Dawn was just starting to break the darkness.

Bolan's mind was racing ahead. If Black Dawn's

lawyer had so much clout, he probably believed he was untouchable. If so, he was about to learn a lesson in humility. When it came to breaking barriers, the Executioner had an unblemished record. His method was simple and direct—locate your target, lock on and don't allow anything or anyone to deter you from that course of action.

3

Bolan was in one of the wealthiest suburbs of Chicago. The garages attached to some of the houses were larger than most ordinary homes. He drove at a steady speed, not wanting to attract attention.

Bolan's target was the residence of Loren Breck, the lawyer who represented Black Dawn. The fact that Breck lived in such a prestigious area confirmed that he was either a damn good lawyer, or he worked for people willing to gamble with the law.

On reaching his hotel, Bolan had showered and dressed in dark pants, black sweater and a soft black leather jacket. He'd called room service and had a light breakfast sent up. While he ate, he had made a call to Breck's office, only to be told that the lawyer wasn't in the office and wasn't expected back until late the following day. On a hunch, Bolan tried the Breck residence. He was told that the lawyer was unable to come to the phone. The soldier hung up, analyzing what it all might mean. Breck might simply be taking the day off, but somehow Bolan didn't think so. Too much had happened in a short space of time.

There was only one way to find out what he was up to.

Arming himself with the 93-R with attached

sound suppressor, his other weapons in the sports bag, Bolan left his room and headed toward the lobby. He picked up a city map from the hotel desk, then made his way to the basement car park. Heading out of the city, Bolan stopped long enough to fill up the rental's tank before picking up the highway that would take him to Lake Forest, through Evanston and Glencoe.

He was still some distance from Lake Forest when he picked up the tail cars. Bolan had been watching his rearview mirror for some time, becoming more convinced he was being followed. He made sure of his suspicions by turning onto a quiet back road, lined on both sides with heavy foliage. And after ten minutes, he spotted his tails. They were hanging back, but they were still there.

Bolan continued driving, reaching a narrower trail that led off the road. It was nothing more than a track. He took it, picking up speed, then swung the car broadside across the roadway and exited the rental, ignition key dropped in his pocket, gun in hand. Ducking low, the soldier dived into the undergrowth and waited.

The first tail car came to a plunging stop, only inches from the rental. A tall man climbed out and studied Bolan's vehicle. Moments later the other vehicle appeared, coming to a halting cloud of dust as the driver jammed on the brakes.

"What the fuck you playing at?" the tall man demanded.

The driver of the second car leaped out, arms waving.

"I almost hit you!"

"Well, you didn't, so quit yelling. If Belasko is still close, he'll figure we're all a bunch of idiots."

"Just remember what Jensen said. This guy is no beginner."

"Yeah? Well, I've been out of kindergarten a long time too," the first man replied.

"Okay, let's move. He's around here somewhere. Can't have gone far. The sooner we take this guy the better."

Bolan counted three in the lead car, two in the second. As the men assembled, they produced automatic pistols. They were gearing up for a manhunt, and the Executioner had a feeling they weren't going to try to take him in alive.

"Let's go!" the tall man said.

The five gunners fanned out from the parked cars and began to search the area.

Bolan had already left his position. He shrank into the undergrowth, first distancing himself from the searchers and then beginning to circle. His plan was to keep beyond the perimeter of their search pattern, moving around them, and ultimately to return to the parked cars from the opposite direction.

The noise from the search party helped Bolan pinpoint them easily. It was obvious they were city types, unused to rural conditions, where the slightest sound carried a long way. To a man like Bolan, who had earned his stripes in the jungles of Southeast Asia, eluding this clumsy crew was achieved without breaking a sweat.

From the cover of thick foliage, Bolan was able to see the three cars. Somewhere behind him he could still hear one of his pursuers, moving back and forth through the undergrowth.

Flicking the Beretta's selector switch to single shot, the soldier leveled the weapon. He used four shots. Each one punctured a tire, two on each car. The moment he triggered the last shot Bolan broke from cover and made a direct run for his own vehicle.

He pulled the key from his pocket with his left hand, keeping the Beretta in the right.

The Executioner was only yards from the car when he saw one of the hit men step out from the undergrowth ahead of him. The guy was between Bolan and his car. For a fraction of a second each man acknowledged the other. Then the subconscious took over and forced the next action.

Bolan dived to the ground, rolling as he heard the clicking sound that signaled that a gun had been fired. The bullet buzzed over his prone body.

Coming to rest on his stomach, Bolan angled the machine pistol's muzzle at the target, gauging the range. The guy had started to run forward.

The 93-R chugged once, then again. The pair of 9 mm Parabellum slugs caught the advancing man in the chest, punching through flesh and muscle to hammer the heart into stillness.

Bolan was on his feet before the dead man hit the ground. He dropped into the driver's seat, calmly slipping the key in the ignition. As he pulled his door shut, he heard raised voices and knew that within a few seconds he'd have company. He heard the engine catch, shifted the car into gear and floored the accelerator. The rental swerved back and forth, shooting dust as it picked up speed along the dirt track. Above the roar of the engine, Bolan heard a barrage of gunshots and felt solid smacks as slugs punctured the vehicle's bodywork. One of the side windows cracked as a projectile bounced off, but it didn't shatter.

Holstering the 93-R, Bolan used both hands to control the wheel, the ruts in the track testing the vehicle's suspension. He rounded a sudden, sharp curve, then felt the track drop away in a steep slope. The gleam of water ahead gave him no more than a few seconds to brace himself as the car hit a shallow stream, almost bottoming out before it raced up the far side with steam swirling from the hot exhaust. Bolan guided the vehicle around another bend, then along an uneven straight before he could ease off the accelerator, bringing the car to a manageable speed.

The track was gradually winding in a curve that would bring him back to the side road and the main highway several miles away. Bolan followed it, and as he drove he reviewed the recent events.

He'd been tailed from Chicago by people who knew his name and were able to pick him up with ease. The opposition had to have information from a reliable source.

Bolan's only hard contact in Chicago had been Hal Brognola, and the police in the form of Ryan Kelly. The soldier backtracked on that. Although Kelly had been the main liaison, there had been others involved—the crew of the patrol car who'd picked him up outside the demolished Black Dawn headquarters and any number of cops inside the precinct.

Bolan also had a name, uttered by one of the armed men from the tail cars.

Jensen.

Who was he? Or she? Some informer who had given the hardmen a description of Bolan and his car? A member of the Chicago PD? Right now Bolan had no idea, but he was going to get Brognola to check it out.

He hit the main highway less than ten minutes later. Bolan checked his position and pushed on. He still had a distance to go. It would give him the opportunity to prepare for whatever lay ahead. He was sure now that Loren Breck would know he was coming, and Bolan could expect a reception committee. That didn't worry him, or make him consider changing his plans. On the contrary. It decided his course of action with even more certainty.

The fact that Black Dawn was prepared to go to such trouble to block his progress meant the organization had something to hide.

And when the enemy became rattled, angry because secrets were likely to be revealed, that was the moment to keep pushing. Hard and fast. Not allowing the opposition time to gather itself and regroup. Bolan's way was to strike and keep striking. Decimating the enemy. Scattering them. Weakening them before moving in for the kill.

4

The rental car was parked off the main road. Bolan, on foot, was skirting the eastern perimeter of the walled estate. It was midafternoon. The bright start to the day had reversed itself, bringing heavy gray clouds that were throwing ominous shadows across the landscape. The weather change was welcome. The vigilance of any sentries posted around the house would be lessened by the onset of cooler weather. Bolan didn't expect an easy ride, but anything that might work in his favor couldn't be discounted.

The soldier crouched in the tangled undergrowth along the high stone wall. He had paced its length, checking it out for alarms or TV cameras. There were no visible signs of any security devices. It was possible that Breck's home was protected by sophisticated sensors that were invisible to the naked eye. Bolan was going to have to rely on instinct. In the normal course of events he would've preferred to check the layout thoroughly before going in. But there wasn't enough time.

He had moved to the farthest point of the eastern wall. Now he crawled along the rear wall, still seeking some point where he could make his incursion.

Bolan spotted the armed guard almost too late.

The sentry, clad in dark pants and a zippered windbreaker, with a suppressed MAC-10 slung from his left shoulder, strode into view from around a clump of tall brush.

His gaze locked on Bolan, and he stared for a silent moment. Then his mouth opened, the beginnings of a shout of alarm.

Bolan kept on moving, closing the short distance quickly, his responses much finer than the guard's. His left hand drove forward, knuckles ramming hard into the guard's throat, choking off the cry. As the guy began to gag, the Executioner slammed the base of his right shoe into his left knee. The impact kicked the guard's leg backward, and he toppled directly into the path of the rising Beretta. The pistol crunched against his lower jaw, pushing his head to one side, blood spraying darkly from split flesh. Bolan rapped the butt of the 93-R against the back of the guard's skull as he sagged to the ground. The soldier took the Ingram, then used the guard's belt to secure his hands behind his back, shoving him deep into the undergrowth.

Moving quickly now the Executioner located the small access gate the guard had used to leave and enter the grounds. It was closed but not locked. Bolan cracked it and slipped through.

The soldier now had the house in his sights. He eased his way through the luxurious greenery of the well-tended gardens. He saw a tennis court and, closer to the house, a swimming pool. Taking cover behind a stone sculpture, the Executioner examined the impressive structure, a testament to wealth and power. A number of expensive cars were parked along the side of the structure, with armed men moving restlessly back and forth between them.

Bolan assessed his chances of getting inside without being spotted. He had no idea how many armed guards were on patrol, but the longer he waited the less his chances.

He waited until the distant figures turned away before making his run for the house, keeping low, using the garden and its ornaments for cover.

The soldier reached the side of the house, his entry point already chosen—a low, flat roof, part of an extension jutting from the main building. Pausing only long enough to stretch and grip the edge of the roof, Bolan hauled himself up and rolled flat. Moving back from the edge, he rose and moved in a crouch to the window he'd targeted.

A quick check showed him an unused bedroom. He scanned the surrounding frame and saw no apparent sensors or wires. Again no guarantee of total safety, but there was no time to hesitate. Bolan used his elbow to break the glass in one pane, then reached in to unlock the catch. The window swung open, and he climbed over the sill. He checked the frame, forcing himself to take time. There was nothing—no sensor plates, no wires. He checked the room fully, and it appeared to be clean.

Bolan crossed to the door and opened it slightly, seeing a wide, expensively furnished hallway, with doors lining both sides. To the right he spotted a wide landing, with a polished wood staircase leading to ground level.

He made sure the hallway was deserted before easing out of the bedroom, the Ingram leading the way. He made it to the landing, pausing as he picked up the low murmur of voices below.

Peering over the banister, he stared into the large entrance hall. Two men in expensive suits, standing by the front door, were having a discussion. One of them had a MAC-10 identical to Bolan's slung by a nylon strap from his shoulder.

A door opened, and a tall, blond man approached the pair. He had a lithe, easy grace about him, and he wore dark pants and a shirt with no tie. He spoke softly to the men. From the way they reacted, he plainly had authority over them. The man with the Ingram turned immediately and headed for the stairs. The other pulled a heavy automatic pistol from beneath his jacket and a compact transceiver from his pocket. He began to talk into it as he moved back and forth across the hall.

The blond man turned and walked away.

The guy with the machine pistol reached the top of the stairs and halted, undecided which way to go next. To his right was the hallway the Executioner had used. An identical one lay to the left. Muttering to himself, the gunman turned right and headed in Bolan's direction.

As the gunner stepped from the landing, turning to check the door to the first room, Bolan stepped into view from the room directly opposite. He closed on the man quickly, angling his left arm around the guard's neck, applying enough pressure to cut off the air supply. At the same time he drove his knee into the man's lower back, savagely smashing the spine. The gunner jerked against the sudden pain, twisting violently to break free. Bolan increased the pressure, turning suddenly to drop into a crouch, pulling the weakening gunman across his raised thigh. The Executioner pushed hard, and his adversary abruptly became still. Lowering him to the floor, the soldier removed the guard's weapon and started to get up.

The whisper of light footsteps sounded behind him. Bolan raised the MAC-10, eyes seeking the source, and came face-to-face with a striking, dark-haired young woman. She wore a black sweater and pants, and in her hands was a matte-black 9 mm Uzi, the muzzle aimed in Bolan's direction.

"Very smooth," the woman said, flicking her gaze from the downed gunman to Bolan. "What do you do for an encore?"

Her accent was German.

Before Bolan could even begin to frame an answer, the house was rocked by a sudden explosive blast.

5

Glass shattered, and the crackle of gunfire filled the air. The sound of shouting—in German as well as English—reached Bolan's ears.

The dark-haired woman was unable to restrain an amused smile as she touched his arm.

"Let's move."

Whatever thoughts went through Bolan's mind at that moment remained there. He had no time to argue with the woman, whomever she was. Action had been forced, and the occupants of the house were resisting. That meant Bolan was involved, like it or not, and he wasn't about to allow himself to become a casualty.

The woman had darted forward, heading for the stairs. As she reached the landing, a door crashed open on the far side, and armed men erupted from the room.

The lead gunner drew on the woman. She dropped to a crouch, triggering a short burst that caught the guy midthigh. He staggered back, crying out in pain as blood spurted from his legs. The wounded man's slide to the floor was aided by a second burst from the SMG that shattered his skull. His partner, forced to step back to avoid his falling companion, tried to bring his own weapon back on-line. Bolan's Ingram coughed harshly, the blast taking the guy in the chest, shredding his heart and lungs. He went down in a bleeding heap.

Backing the woman as she hit the stairs, Bolan followed her down. The suit in the hall dropped his transceiver and raced toward the foot of the stairs, raking the pair with a burst from his MAC-10. Splinters of wood filled the air as the bullets chewed at the banister.

Bolan and the woman both turned their weapons on the gunner at the same time, the force of their combined volley lifting him off his feet and spinning him into the wall. He lost his balance and fell facedown, his body racked by violent spasms.

From outside the house came the continuing barrage of small-arms fire, the sound of engines revving wildly and tires screeching.

The door to their left, across the hall, stood ajar. Thick tendrils of white smoke drifted from beneath the threshold. As Bolan reached the ground floor, the door was flung open and a blond man stumbled into the hall, coughing, and pawing at his eyes with one hand as his other waved an automatic pistol. As his watering eyes made out the hazy figures of Bolan and the woman, he began to trigger wild shots in their direction.

The woman dropped into a crouch, her finger stroking the Uzi's trigger. Her burst drilled into the blonde's midsection, and he stumbled back, a look of astonishment on his face. Blood began to spread across the front of his shirt. He collapsed in a sprawl, dying without a sound.

Dark-clad figures toting Uzis rushed through the door. They acknowledged the woman, looking beyond her to Bolan. Their firearms began to rise until she lifted a hand.

"He's a friendly," she stated simply, and the weapons were lowered. "What have you found?"

One of the men shook his head. "Nothing that's of interest to us."

"Resistance?"

"Some. We took care of it. There were a few who broke out."

"We have to look for Benjamin," the woman said.

"Maybe the basement."

"Yes."

"Is that Benjamin Meyer?" Bolan asked.

All eyes turned on him.

"What do you know?" the woman asked harshly, clutching at Bolan's arm. There was anger in her face, but the look in her eyes told a different story. "Please."

"He's dead," Bolan told her, his voice gentle. "I found him yesterday in Chicago."

"Theresa, we should move on. If Ben isn't here, then we have nothing to keep us."

The woman glanced at the speaker. She ran a hand through her thick mane of dark hair, shaking her head as if to clear her mind. Then she nodded.

"Clear the place," she said. "Then we go."

She turned to stare at Bolan, scanning his face, reaching out to touch him again.

"I need to talk with you. Will you come with us?"

Bolan nodded and turned to the waiting men. "Was the lawyer, Breck, in there?"

"You saw him in the hall. The blond man."

"He won't be putting any more of these Nazi hoodlums back on the streets," one of the others added.

There was no need to ask further questions. Loren Breck had paid his dues for consorting with the neo-Nazi group. It appeared that the Executioner wasn't the only one dispensing justice this day.

"Ten minutes," the woman said sharply. "See what information you can find. After that we leave."

When they were momentarily alone, Bolan turned to the woman.

"I have a car back along the road. It has equipment I need."

She nodded. "We'll pick it up on the way out."

The gunfire outside had stopped. Silence fell.

The woman crossed to the main door and pulled it wide open. She stood looking outside, into the falling rain. Bolan watched her, saw the slump of her shoulders and her head drop forward. He left her in her moment of grief. Whomever Benjamin Meyer had been, it was clear he meant a great deal to this woman. There were no words to cover a time like this, no way of easing the pain, or lessening the loss. Bolan had been through that personal hell, and he chose to allow the woman her moment.

WITHIN TWENTY MINUTES they were driving away from the silent house. The lady and her four-man team were using an unobtrusive, two-year-old Chrysler. They circled the drive that fronted the house, bypassing the dead guards, and cruised to the gates. Taking a left, she followed Bolan's directions and drove to where he had concealed his car. The Executioner started the rental, pulled onto the road and followed the others back the way they had come. After leaving the Breck house behind, they drove steadily for the next two hours, finally reaching the team's base.

Once the vehicles had been parked and all the equipment transferred inside the base house, the woman sat with Bolan to exchange information.

The first thing Bolan learned was her name: Theresa Meyer.

The dead man he had found in the basement of the Black Dawn headquarters in Chicago had been her brother.

6

"My brother wasn't trained for combat," Theresa Meyer said. "He was an activist, yes, but his talents lay in the art of politics and science. Benjamin was a talker."

"He was working undercover according to my information," Bolan explained.

"I only found out myself a short time ago. Benjamin had disappeared. No one could figure out where he was. Until a week ago. Word came through that he had been recognized by one of our people in Austria. He was with Black Dawn, at one of their meeting places. Of course there were many rumors, that he had defected, gone over to the enemy."

"You didn't believe that?" Bolan asked.

"Never. Black Dawn represents everything Ben despised. Nazi ideology—the evil we hoped had died in Berlin when Hitler was killed. But there are still many in Germany who cling to the ideals. They want to try again. There's support for them in certain quarters, with enough of the old Nazis around to keep the fires burning. And to pass the torch to a new generation."

"Racists? Political activists? One country, one people?"

Meyer nodded. "They play on the basest of human prejudice. They use unemployment, alien cheap labor and resentment of the affluent classes—all extremely emotional issues."

"Was that the platform they used when they tried to get their people elected to local government?"

"Yes. Small beginnings. If they could get a toe-hold in small-town politics, it would have allowed them to plan for higher offices later."

"But it didn't work?"

"This time around the Black Dawn candidates came in at the bottom of the polls. But the indications are that given time they might achieve their aims."

"How did you become involved?"

The woman's dark eyes flashed. "Getting involved is easy. Staying objective is the hard part. I was with the German police—antiterrorist squad. Certain aspects of policy didn't go down too well with me, so in the end I quit and went back to standard policing. Shortly after I was recruited into a covert unit. This was government sponsored, but in so deep it didn't exist on paper. Our job was to infiltrate and disrupt, by any means, organizations presenting a threat to the stability of the nation. One of the targets was Black Dawn. We'd been working on the main group for almost six months when I found out that Benjamin was involved. We hadn't seen each other for some time. So it was a shock when I learned my own brother had infiltrated Black Dawn. I found out from one of Ben's friends that they had suspicions Black Dawn was working on some kind of terror weapon. They were going to use it to hit back against the government they felt had conspired to ruin their chances of fielding candidates for election. Ben had stayed with the group to try and find out more. We didn't find out he had moved to America with them until a week ago.''

''He'd been feeding my people information on Black Dawn's activities for a few weeks. He gave us the background that brought me in. But too late to help him.''

''I can hardly believe we're talking about my brother. I just never imagined him doing anything like this.''

''He was a brave man, Theresa.''

''And this mysterious weapon theory we've been trying to identify? Is it all linked together?''

''We're both after the same terrorist group,'' Bolan said. ''We heard that the U.S. Black Dawn was planning a merger with the German wing to increase their overall strength and give them more of a presence. This weapon you mentioned. Any idea what it is?''

Meyer shook her head. ''No. We heard only vague rumors that it would be something no one would be able to combat. Have you found anything?''

''Maybe,'' Bolan said.

''Anything we could use?''

''Nothing solid. Only a few leads we haven't tied together yet.''

Meyer banged her fist on the table, her frustration evident. And also the pain she was suffering now that the death of her brother had been confirmed—coming this far only to be told there was nothing she could do because she was too late.

''Theresa, if there was anything I could do to

make this easier, believe me, I would. But as nicely as I wrap it up, Benjamin is still dead. The only consolation is that the people who did it won't walk away.''

Bolan decided not to detail the way Benjamin Meyer had died. If the truth came out later, she would deal with it in her own way.

''Thank you, Mike. It's harder for me because I can't even step forward to claim the body. We're not supposed to be here. Our operation is not sanctioned.''

Bolan understood better than Theresa would ever know. His own war, from its inception, had been outside the law, and there were still times when he operated by his rules in order to complete a mission. Theresa and her team had followed their instincts. If it took a little bending the rules to put a stop to whatever was being planned, then Mack Bolan had no objections.

''Theresa, I need to get back to Chicago. I have to talk to my people and follow up on a few leads. I'll pass along any information that might be helpful to you. But lay low for a while, until you hear from me.''

Meyer considered his words for a few moments, exchanging glances with her companions. There was a general murmur of agreement.

''All right, Mike. We'll stay here until we hear from you. But don't make it too long.''

BOLAN PULLED into a service station and located a pay phone. When the receiver was picked up, it was Ryan Kelly's voice on the line.

"Hey, pal, we got worried when you did your vanishing act."

"Is Brognola there?"

"Stepped out to get a breath of air. The guy looks like he needs a week's sleep. You come up with anything?"

"You haven't heard over the wire?"

"Should I?"

"Long story, Kelly, but Breck's place was hit. I'd just gone in myself and got caught up in it. Breck didn't come out alive."

"Damn," the cop said. "So no chance to talk to him?"

"No. Kelly, I'm on my way in. Just a word. Somebody set a tail on me from the city. I handled it but a name came up. Jensen. Does it mean anything?"

Bolan heard Kelly's sharp intake of breath and knew he'd hit close to home.

"Oh, yeah. It means something."

7

Kurt Mohn waited until the room was empty. As the door closed behind the tall figure of Klaus Erlich, leaving Mohn alone, he turned to stare out the window. Hands clasped behind his back, he watched as the three men emerged from the house and walked to their cars.

They were all driving American automobiles, huge monsters that glittered in the bright sunlight. Long, low-slung vehicles with fat tires and soft seats, the cars were evidence of the way the men had embraced the American dream, the materialistic trophies of an indulgent society. Weak and pliable.

Mohn's eyes were cold, devoid of expression.

How he hated them.

Behind him the door opened and closed with barely a sound. He picked up the faint sound and turned to confront the tall blond man.

"Not a true German among them," he said softly.

"Living in America has weakened them," Erlich stated.

"Living in America has destroyed them. Blinded them. They see only what they want to see."

"But we need them," Erlich added.

"For their contacts and the influence. Yes, I know, but I feel contaminated by them."

A slow smile formed on Mohn's lips. "When we're done with them, I think we'll *contaminate* them. What do you think, Klaus?"

"Excellent idea. Let them feel what real power means."

Erlich crossed to where a coffee percolator bubbled gently. He poured two cups of the rich, aromatic brew, passing one to the man by the window.

"Despite my personal feelings about them, Klaus, I have to agree with them on certain points. We haven't done ourselves any favors with the disappointing performances over the past few days. First that fiasco in Nevada. The best opportunity we could've had to demonstrate the virus, and it was all lost. Then the foolishness in Chicago. Apart from the embarrassment of discovering an informer within the organization, we've lost the premises, and our people have been forced to scatter."

"They've relocated at the gun club," Erlich reminded him.

"What's more disturbing is the attack on Breck's home and his death."

This time it was Erlich who passed off the lawyer's death with a shrug.

"Breck's long-term usefulness was over. I think we both knew that. Our late comrade was starting to cast an envious eye in the direction of your seat of command."

"Klaus, I do believe you're becoming as cynical as I am."

"I take that as a compliment."

"Do we have any details on who was responsible for the attack on the Chicago base and Breck's home?"

"Nothing definite. Only what our people saw before they escaped. Some kind of hit team. Not official I'd say. Perhaps friends of Benjamin Meyer trying to find him. There appears to be some kind of information blackout. The only lead came from Jensen, our police informer. Even that was thin. We have a name. Mike Belasko. No more. Jensen had one of our backup teams follow him. But he staged an ambush, disabled their cars and shot one of the men before he moved on, apparently in the direction of Breck's place. By the time we received the information, the attack had taken place and Breck was dead."

Mohn sighed, turning to sit behind the desk that stood near the window. He placed the cup of coffee in front of him, his expression thoughtful.

"I choose to believe that Meyer got information out before he died. I'm also certain he told us the truth, that his suspicions about us were limited. He had some idea we were planning something, but he wasn't sure what. Which means the authorities won't know what to look for."

"Unless they find some evidence."

Mohn smiled. "Kolbe?"

"Yes."

"For all his faults at least Corbin followed instructions and burned the body."

"Medical examiners in this country have extremely sophisticated techniques to fall back on."

"You're correct. It's well within the bounds of possibility that the Americans may find something. We have to be prepared for setbacks. Time to retreat to home base and direct operations from there. What do you think?"

"I think we can handle that," Erlich agreed. "The operations center is virtually complete. We could bring it on-line within a few more days if we work around the clock."

Mohn considered the proposal.

"Start making arrangements. In the meantime, I'll speak to Jensen and make sure he understands we need more information. I want to know who has been upsetting our plans. The more we know the sooner we can deal with him."

"I'll get things under way," Erlich said and left the room.

Mohn finished his coffee and picked up the telephone. He punched a number, then sat back while it rang.

"I need to talk."

The voice on the other end of the line was agitated.

"Not on this line. Give me ten minutes, and I'll call you back."

"I'll be waiting."

Mohn replaced the receiver. He swung his comfortable chair around so he could look out the window. His gaze lifted to see the distant range of low hills—soft purple in the heat haze, a ragged line that separated land from sky. They had an extremely calming effect on Mohn, drawing him into a mood of quiet reflection. A time of assessment.

His longterm plans hadn't changed. Kurt Mohn believed passionately in his concept of global domination by a single, all-embracing power. It could be achieved.

His way.

Mohn's way was clean and efficient. His Armageddon Virus would strike terror into millions of hearts because of its sheer simplicity. The beauty of the virus lay in its silent, unseen capability to kill.

No warning. No chaos. It could happen anywhere. At any time—on a crowded city street, in a rural community or on a moving train. There were those who'd argue that an explosive device would achieve the same, and to a point they were right. But a bomb had to be manufactured and then transported to its target. Mohn's virus was carried in a slender tube that could be disguised as a pen and taken into places no bomber could reach. The carrier would then calmly slip away without attracting attention, enabling him to be at a safe distance when the container released its charge. The full horror of the Armageddon Virus would be realized as the victims began to react, exhibiting the ravaging symptoms before death claimed them, and all taking place in full view of those around them.

Mohn's campaign would begin with a few selected targets, and as the pressure was applied the Black Dawn carriers would activate a wider reaching demonstration. Targets would be picked randomly across the country, highlighting America's vulnerability. Over a sustained period, dozens of attacks would be staged until the U.S. continent was at Mohn's mercy. The American military would be helpless, unable to retaliate. What use were fleets of heavily laden bombers? Columns of tanks? The mighty U.S. Navy? The whole nation could be brought to its knees by Mohn's invisible army. No one would know where or when the next attack would be.

At the same time a parallel campaign would take

place in Germany. Black Dawn would duplicate the operation. The attacks would serve as a prelude to a concentrated campaign by the organization, rallying as many of the right-wing groups joined Black Dawn and initiated a resurgence of German dominance in Europe.

Mohn believed it could work.

He had to. If he had doubts, he couldn't expect his followers to remain faithful.

He recalled his late father's words: Be faithful unto death! And beyond!

Joachim Mohn had instilled those beliefs in his son, educating him in the all-encompassing lore of Adolf Hitler's Third Reich. And Kurt Mohn had become the Aryan clone in word and deed.

He still had his father's SS belt buckle, and lived out the legend inscribed on the smooth, worn metal.

Meine Ehre heisst Treue—My Honor Is Loyalty.

It had always been, and would remain, the force that kept him on his unswerving path despite setbacks.

It had sustained him through the destruction of his Amazon stronghold and his first attempt to launch the Armageddon Virus on an unsuspecting world. Mohn's defeat at the hands of a team of American combat specialists had forced him to go on the run.

Luck had played a great part in Mohn's survival. Luck and foresight. Before he went ahead with the processing of the virus at his Amazon base, Mohn had duplicated all research data on computer disks and had a set lodged with an old friend of his late father's. As well as the disks, Mohn had active samples of the virus in sealed units, stored at low temperature. Once he was satisfied that he was no longer being pursued, Mohn had visited his old friend and had taken possession of his property. Within weeks Mohn had recruited new biochemists from within the Nazi network and set up his new development base—this time in America itself, the most fitting place for his power base. Right at the heart of Western democracy.

It was the best place for Kurt Mohn to orchestrate his scheme, to gather his faceless army and prepare for the day when Black Dawn would rise.

THE TELEPHONE RANG, breaking Mohn's reverie. He turned toward the desk and picked up the receiver.

"Are you feeling less paranoid now?" Mohn asked after the caller identified himself.

"Easy for you to say. What am I supposed to do? Take your call in the goddamn squad room?"

"And there I was believing you were genuine in wanting to help the cause."

"Cut the crap. Helping is one thing. Being suicidal is for the fucking kamikaze pilots."

"Jensen, listen. The attack on Breck's home and his subsequent death leave some loose ends that require securing. There isn't much we can do about information he might have had at his house, though I doubt even Breck would've been so careless as to take incriminating documents home. On the other hand, his office is another matter. Get over there as soon as you can. Remove anything that might cause the group embarrassment. Understand?"

"Yeah. Leave it to me."

"And take some backup with you. Just in case." Mohn hesitated. "We're going to move dates forward. Just as a precaution. When you have cleared Breck's office call me again and I'll update you.''

"No problem," Jensen replied. "I'm moving now.''

Mohn replaced the receiver. He sat staring at it, trying to decide on the cop. His attitude didn't seem correct. It would necessitate watching. The man was useful, being a part of the Chicago PD. He was well placed to pick up on anything that might prove threatening to Black Dawn. His familiarity with American policing methods allowed him the opportunity to pass along information. Now all he had to do was to make Breck's office safe.

Mohn stood. It was time to abandon this compound and return to their main base. Once there, he could concentrate on preparing for the first demonstrations of the Armageddon Virus. Then he could watch America start to panic.

8

Hal Brognola returned to the office minutes after Bolan's call. Kelly related the conversation he'd had with the Executioner, and the big Fed immediately put through a call to Stony Man.

Kelly, meanwhile, wandered down to the squad room. Helping himself to a cup of coffee from the machine in the corner, he watched Stan Jensen take a telephone call at his desk. Jensen seemed agitated about something, breaking off the call quickly. He sat at his desk for a moment, then snatched up his coat and made his way out of the department. Kelly followed at a distance and wasn't surprised to see the cop stop at a pay phone. Jensen completed his call, hung up, then made a second one. This was shorter, and once he'd completed it he turned back the way he'd come. Before following him, Kelly crossed to the pay phone and checked the number on the machine, making a note of the time as well. He caught up with Jensen as the man went directly to his parked car outside the police building. Reaching his own vehicle, Kelly fired up the engine and pulled into the traffic about four cars behind the dirty cop.

They drove across town, the pace slow due to the late-afternoon traffic. Kelly saw where they were heading, and the realization simply confirmed his suspicion about Stan Jensen. A while later they were on the fringes of the business district. Jensen took a couple of turns and pulled his car to the curb, where he sat staring through his windshield at the building directly in front of him. After a couple of minutes, he climbed out of his vehicle and cut across the street.

Kelly parked down the street, sat watching Jensen as the cop entered the building that housed Loren Breck's office.

Damn Jensen, Kelly thought angrily. It looked like Belasko had been right and the man was in bed with Black Dawn.

Jumping out of his car, Kelly ran across the street, dodging traffic and ignoring the blare of horns. His mind was on what might lie ahead. He entered the building and paused just inside the high glass doors long enough to allow Jensen to enter one of the elevators. Kelly knew which floor housed the lawyer's suite of offices. He saw Jensen's car stop at Breck's floor and made his way over to one of the other elevators. His car was empty. As it started to rise, Kelly took out his handgun and made sure the safety was off before he returned the Beretta 92-F to its holster on his right hip.

The car stopped. As the doors slid open, Kelly peered into the corridor. It was quiet at that time of day. A number of the offices were vacant. The building was fairly new, and a lot of floor space was still available for rent. Kelly stepped out and walked toward Breck's office. The door stood slightly open. Easing his Beretta from its holster, the policeman touched the door and let it swing open. There was an outer office, with a receptionist. A young woman lay on the floor beside the main desk, her blond hair spread out across the carpet where she lay. Blood streaked her pale face and ran through her hair, soaking into the carpet. Kelly bent over her briefly, checking her pulse. It was there—uneven but at least there. He stood, then walked stealthily across the reception area and flattened himself against the double doors that led into the main office.

Kelly could hear hurried movements inside the office, someone opening drawers, checking the contents. Every so often he would pick up the low monotone of Jensen's voice as the cop failed to locate whatever he was seeking.

Kelly closed his left hand over the door handle and eased it open a fraction, peering through the gap to scan the office. Directly across from the door was a wide picture window that offered a view of the city. Breck's large, black desk and chair stood in front of the window section. Expensive art hung on the beige walls.

A flicker of movement caught Kelly's eye, and Jensen moved into view. The dirty cop had a sheaf of papers in his hands and he was going through the bundle, discarding whatever he didn't want. Sheets fluttered to the carpeted floor, then Jensen hurled the whole sheaf aside with a muttered curse. He turned abruptly, stalked across to a bank of filing cabinets and began dragging open the drawers and pulling files. His search took on a frantic note as he failed to locate whatever it was he sought.

Kelly had seen enough. He slipped into the office, standing with his back to the door.

"I hope to hell you got a warrant for all this, Stan."

Jensen's hand froze in midair, still holding the file he'd just pulled from a drawer. Only his head turned as he looked back over his shoulder and met Kelly's angry stare.

"What you doing here, Ryan?" he asked, his tone almost casual.

"Turns out I'm on a rat hunt," Kelly said, making no attempt to disguise his feelings.

"Damned Irish shithead," Jensen yelled.

He turned from the cabinet, hurling the thick file at Kelly, then broke to the left. Jensen threw himself across the top of the wide desk, sliding over the polished surface and rolling out of sight on the far side.

Kelly batted aside the file, swinging around his Beretta to pick up on Jensen. Too late. The man had dropped from sight.

The black muzzle of a handgun appeared over the edge of the desk, followed by Jensen's head. He stroked the trigger, firing a single shot. The slug missed Kelly by inches and embedded itself in the wall behind him. The dirty cop kept triggering, sending shot after shot after Kelly as he pulled back.

The bullet that did hit him knocked him to his knees. Kelly let out a gasp of pain, his breath catching in his lungs as the heavy slug grazed a rib. He clamped his left hand over the ragged wound, feeling hot blood seep through his fingers. He pushed himself across the carpet, desperately seeking cover, and rolled behind a large leather couch.

"Come on out, you fucking bog Irish mother!"

Jensen yelled. "I want to see that ugly mug when I plant a bullet in it."

Kelly dragged himself to the far end of the couch, aware that his position was critical. The couch wasn't going to offer cover for long, and it wasn't going to stop any bullets Jensen might fire his way.

Suddenly, there was a crash as the dirty cop emerged from behind the desk, throwing aside the leather chair.

Taking a deep breath and choking off a groan of pain, Kelly forced himself to his knees. He shoved the Beretta in front of him as he raised his head just above the back of the couch. He saw Jensen stepping around the edge of the desk, his face dark with rage, eyes scanning the office.

Kelly tracked him with the 92-F, pulling the trigger the moment he had Jensen in his sights. The 9 mm slug tore a chunk from his left shoulder, spinning him 180 degrees. Jensen fell back against the desk, his mouth spitting obscenities, as he brought his own weapon around. Kelly triggered twice, driving a pair of 9 mm projectiles into the crooked cop's chest. Jensen slammed back, his face registering surprise. His finger jerked on the trigger of his revolver, pumping a slug into the side of the desk. Kelly followed through and cut loose with two more shots. One caught Jensen in the lower throat, blood immediately pumping out of the dark, round entry hole. He began to choke. The second slug hit him in the center of his chest. He slid to his knees, dropping his gun as he tried to staunch the stream of blood from soaking the front of his shirt. He slumped at the base of the desk, leaning against it, head sagging forward.

Kelly dragged himself across the carpet, keeping his Beretta on the crooked cop even though the man was unlikely to do anything. He reached out and scooped up Jensen's gun, throwing it across the room. The pain from his wound was increasing, and Kelly had to pause to pull himself together.

He felt Jensen's eyes on him. The man had one hand pressed tightly against his throat, trying to stop the bleeding.

"Had to interfere, didn't you?" Jensen rasped. His voice was barely audible, and the words came out in bubbles of bloody froth. "You won't stop anything. Not now...too fucking late..."

A whisper of sound reached Kelly's ears. It was the door opening behind him. He heard the soft click of a safety being released.

He dropped and rolled.

The office vibrated to the harsh chatter of autofire, and Kelly felt the impact of the bullets as they whacked into the floor only inches from his moving body.

He came to rest on his back, shoving himself to a half-sitting position, the barrel of the Beretta already tracking the source of the gunfire.

A stocky figure clad in a long leather coat stood in the office doorway, a stubby Ingram clenched in his fists. The muzzle was already moving along the line of bullet holes in the floor, closing in on Kelly's prone figure.

A wild jumble of thoughts and emotions filled the cop's head as he jerked the Beretta into target acquisition and fired. He felt the 92-F buck in his fist, and just kept on firing until the pistol's slide locked back on an empty breech.

As Kelly released the empty clip and fumbled for his spare, he heard a deep, almost inhuman sound. Forcing himself to finish loading the Beretta, he shook his head to clear away the fog and turned to find the source of the sound.

The guy in the leather coat was slumped awkwardly against the doorframe, the Ingram hanging loosely from the fingers of his right hand. He was sliding to the floor. On his knees, he stretched out his left hand as if begging for some kind of help. Most of Kelly's slugs had hit him in the upper chest, neck and head. The leather coat was slick with blood. The left side of his face was torn and bloody. Two of Kelly's hits had taken away most of his lower jaw and cheekbone. He fell facedown suddenly, as if his strength had evaporated, and he lay on the carpet, still moaning.

Climbing to his feet Kelly moved to the desk and retrieved the telephone Jensen had knocked to the floor. He punched in a number and waited until it was answered.

"Kelly," he said when Hal Brognola's voice came on the line. "You want to work some of that federal magic? Then get on over to Breck's office, but bring medical help, too. There are three down and I stopped one myself."

"Kelly, you hang on," Brognola said. "We're on our way."

The cop put the phone down, starting to feel weak. He looked at Jensen. The man had stopped breathing. Easing his way around to the leather seat behind the desk, Kelly slumped into it. He was able to see the door from there, and he kept the Beretta aimed at it. All he needed to do now was stay awake until the cavalry arrived.

9

Bolan had cleaned up and was just about to leave when the telephone rang. He picked it up and heard Hal Brognola's weary tones on the other end of the line.

"You ready to move out?" the big Fed asked.

"Yeah."

"I'll pick you up in twenty minutes. Leave the rental in the hotel garage. I'll have it picked up."

"Talk session coming up?"

Brognola chuckled. "Something like that."

"Okay. I'll wait downstairs."

Bolan had showered and changed into fresh clothing on his return to Chicago. The trip back had been uneventful, but he couldn't shake off the feeling he might still be under surveillance. Black Dawn seemed to have an efficient network. The example of Stan Jensen was one that couldn't be ignored. If the Nazi group had a cop on their payroll, who else was working for them behind a mask of respectability?

The Executioner's thoughts returned to Ryan Kelly. He had dropped by the hospital to see the cop on his return to the city, having learned of Kelly's wounding from Brognola when he'd checked in. The cop had greeted Bolan with a smile.

"Walked into it like a damn rookie," he'd admitted.

"Important thing is that you walked out alive and the bad guys didn't," Bolan said. "I've had a few surprises myself this time round."

Kelly checked out Bolan's clothing, still showing the signs of his encounter at Breck's home.

"Sneaky bastards, these Nazis. Got to admit they're organized when it comes to protecting their backs."

"What about Jensen?"

"Stan? He was a hard-nosed son of a bitch. Never had much time for anyone if they didn't come up to his standards."

"Like?"

"White. All-American. Stan never made any secret about how he felt, but he never overplayed it when he was working. He did his job within the law. I never figured him for an out-and-out bigot. Jesus, I'd have laughed at anyone if they'd told me he was into this Nazi crap."

"It has an appeal for a lot of people, Kelly. The ideology pulls in all kinds."

"So where do you go from here?"

"Go back to my hotel, clean up, then figure my next move."

"You might want to snoop around Jensen's place," the cop suggested. "Who knows?"

He gave Bolan the address.

"Take care, Kelly."

"Sure enough. Keep me posted, Belasko."

BROGNOLA ARRIVED ON TIME. They went out to his car, the Justice man slipping behind the wheel and easing into traffic.

"I'm taking the next flight back. I figure I can do more for you from Stony Man. I need to talk to some people in Germany. The way this thing is widening out, Black Dawn could be about to raise hell over there as well. The sooner we alert the authorities the better."

"Maybe they can send some information our way," Bolan suggested.

"Striker, just what the hell happened at Breck's place?" Brognola asked.

Bolan related the whole thing, from the moment Theresa Meyer and her team had shown up. The big Fed listened in silence, allowing Bolan to complete his briefing before he spoke.

"Ties in with some murmurs we've been getting via the other agencies about the possibility of a foreign strike team on American soil. Up until now, I didn't have any idea which side they were working on."

"How do we know the rumors were about Theresa Meyer and her team? Maybe they were fingering Black Dawn. Could be the German group sent over some reinforcements."

Brognola digested the possibility.

"I'll have Aaron run a series of trawls through the information net and see what he can come up with. If there's anything, he'll dredge it up one way or another."

"Did you keep a lid on Jensen's death?"

Brognola nodded. "Why?"

"I have a visit planned to his home. I might turn up something."

"Worth a try."

At O'Hare Brognola turned the car over to Bolan.

"Looks less suspicious than yours," he said. "No bullet holes in it." Then he smiled. "Not yet anyway."

"Be in touch," Bolan said.

He headed back to the city. The address Kelly had given him was in one of the residential areas built on the city fringes some years earlier. By the time Bolan had driven through the early-evening traffic, it was starting to get dark. The rainy weather was still around, though now it had reduced to a slight, persistent drizzle.

The wooden houses on the street where Jensen had lived were identical, a study in cheap urban construction. Bolan pulled to a stop at the curb just short of the cop's unlit house and studied the layout. Each house was enclosed by wooden fencing, with lawns fronting them. Jensen's grass didn't look as if it had been cut for some time.

Before leaving the car Bolan checked his Beretta 93-R. He crossed the sidewalk and moved quickly across the lawn and down the side of the house. He pulled into the shadows at the back and looked it over. There were no signs that suggested Jensen had done anything to improve security. Bolan made a quick observation of the windows. He found a small fanlight open and used it to reach inside to unlock the main window. After climbing through, he closed the window behind him.

Taking out the 93-R, Bolan took a slow look around what appeared to be a bedroom. The bed itself was unmade. A crumpled shirt and pants were thrown across the bed. Others were draped on a chair. It seemed Jensen lived alone. There were no signs of any female clothing in the wardrobe, nor anywhere else in the room. Bolan moved on. The next room was a second bedroom, but it had been converted into a study.

The room was furnished with a cheap desk and a scarred wooden file cabinet. A shelf above the desk held a number of books—a couple about guns, a history of the Third Reich, a manual on urban terrorism and a cheaply printed volume detailing the need to cleanse America of the ethnic impurities in society.

The file cabinet held a selection of Black Dawn propaganda and magazines, leaflets and tracts glorifying the policies of Black Dawn and what it could do to save America. Bolan scanned the leaflets, dumping them back in the cabinet with a shake of his head. The problem was that a lot of people would read the Black Dawn claims and sympathize with them, while others would be encouraged to take real action by joining the group.

Bolan searched the desk, which seemed to hold nothing but personal papers. A number of bank statements showed that Jensen had barely lived within his police salary. The Executioner was closing one of the drawers when he felt it catch. Pulling it completely out, he turned it over and saw a manila envelope taped to the underside. The flap had come loose and was catching whenever the drawer closed. The soldier pulled the envelope free, tipping the contents onto a cleared space on the desktop.

There was a bank passbook that showed that the account holder, named Steve Petrie, had been receiving monthly payments for almost twelve months. The total amount in the account, even after a number of withdrawals, was close to $50,000.

A sheet of paper was folded inside the passbook. On it were a few names and telephone numbers. Bolan recognized only two of the names: Asher Kolbe and Leo Corbin.

The dead men found in the desert outside Las Vegas.

Bolan pocketed the two items.

He made a quick search of the rest of the house, finding nothing of interest. The soldier left the house and returned to his car. As he was unlocking his door, he picked up the soft sound of an idling car engine. Bolan made no outward sign of having heard the noise. He glanced in the direction of the vehicle without turning his head, and saw a dark-colored sedan moving slowly across the street, coming up alongside his parked car. The headlights were turned off. Peering through his own rear window, Bolan saw a dark shape leaning out of the sedan's front passenger window, and despite the gloom he also made out the shape of a stubby submachine gun in the hit man's hands.

He didn't wait any longer.

Exiting through the passenger door, he ducked below the level of the car roof and pulled out the Beretta. As he dropped, he heard suppressed autofire. The stream of slugs pounded the rental's bodywork. Glass shattered, and the car rocked under the impacts.

Bolan moved to the rear of the car. He heard the squeal of tires as the sedan accelerated, pulling away from his vehicle. Standing, the Executioner leaned across the rental's roof, the 93-R braced in both hands. He squeezed off a couple of 3-round bursts, drilling a number of 9 mm projectiles into the upper body of the gunner. The guy fell back inside the sedan. Stepping around the back of his car, Bolan tracked the Beretta on the retreating sedan and triggered again, blowing out the rear window. The car lurched, swinging across the street and colliding with the rear of a parked paneled van. It came to a dead stop, the engine stalling.

The Executioner moved back to his own vehicle, slipping behind the wheel. He fired up the engine, calmly turned the car around and drove away from Jensen's house. He couldn't be sure there weren't others around, maybe a backup team waiting in case he had survived the first attempt. One thing Bolan was sure of. Black Dawn seemed to have a solid supply of guns lurking in the shadows.

He watched his mirrors all the way back to the city, taking a circuitous route to his hotel, and even then he didn't feel entirely secure. The opposition had a knack of being well-informed. It was possible they knew where he was staying by now. He parked on the street outside the hotel, checking the area. It was completely dark now, so a one-hundred-percent guarantee he wasn't being watched would be difficult to gauge. He weighed the need for caution against his need to contact Stony Man, and decided that wherever he went in Chicago, the enemy could follow.

He left the car and went inside. At the reception desk he asked if he could use the hotel's fax machine. The clerk took him to the small room set aside for guests' business needs. Bolan keyed in the number that would connect him to Stony Man, via a series of cutouts, and fed in the sheet holding the names and telephone numbers. As the fax transmitted the information, Bolan picked up the telephone, attached a portable scrambler device and punched in the Farm's number. When the call connected, Bolan spoke to Barbara Price.

"You okay?" she asked.

"I'm fine."

"Is this an update?"

"I'll get to that. There should be a fax coming through. I need a check on the names and numbers. And take down this bank-account information." He read off the account number and the name. "Have the Bear run this through his system."

"Will do."

"The man is on his way home," Bolan advised. "I dropped him at the airport awhile back."

"You still engaged out there?"

"Long way to go yet."

"We have some feedback from the coroner in Vegas. He did an in-depth autopsy on Kolbe. The man did die from exposure to some ultrapowerful virus."

"Any details on it?"

"Negative. Apparently it isn't readily identifiable as a known virus strain."

"Something new? Man-made?"

"Can't say yet. The medical examiner says it appears to have unusual characteristics. He's contacting the Centers for Disease Control in Atlanta for help to identify it."

"I'll talk to you later," Bolan said and hung up.

He didn't need to go to his room because his bag was already in the car. It was time to move on, to stay mobile. He went back to his rental and drove away from the hotel. Not signing out would perhaps leave the impression he might be returning. It was a small point, but it might tie up a few of the enemy, keep them off his back while he formulated his next move.

Bolan drove across the city until he eventually located a diner and parked. Going inside, he found a pay phone and dialed the number Theresa Meyer had given to him. He felt he needed to talk to her, if only to reassure her that he hadn't abandoned her completely.

The number connected at the other end and rang. For too long.

10

"Tarrant has located them," Klaus Erlich said, a note of triumph in his voice.

"The strike team?" Mohn asked, smiling when Erlich nodded. "It's time we had some good news."

"The information came from one of the informants Jensen put us on to."

"Is the man Belasko with them?" Mohn asked.

"He was, but he has left them."

Mohn fell silent, considering his options.

"A suggestion," Klaus ventured.

"Yes?"

"The quicker we remove this team the better," Erlich said. "We can do it within the next couple of hours."

"Where is this leading, Klaus?"

"A chance for us to be noticed. A practical demonstration of the virus. To make up for the missed opportunity in Las Vegas. You want to show the Americans what's in store for them. So let's make full use of this occasion. Give the authorities something to worry about. A taste of what is to come. Using the virus will do that and also rid us of this damned strike team. Something for the idiots back in Germany to take heed of, a warning shot that says this will happen to anyone who tries to interfere. Use the virus to eliminate the strike team, then an anonymous call to the police and the media, pointing them to the scene. We might even make the six-o'clock news.''

Mohn smiled, then chuckled.

''I like it, Klaus,'' he said. ''Who will you use? Tarrant?''

''He's the only choice at the moment. He won't fail us. I can have him here in half an hour.''

''Good! Do it. I'll prepare the virus for him. Once he's on the move we can shut down here. Everything is ready.''

TARRANT PARKED THE CAR and sat watching the distant house. It stood back from the quiet back road, an old wooden building standing on a low hill, with a few trees forming a windbreak on the north side. The trees interested Tarrant because they would give him cover as he made his approach. To be certain there were no outside guards, he spent a good twenty minutes scanning the area. Finally satisfied, he reached over the rear seat and grabbed the zippered bag.

Inside was a protective biohazard suit fitted with a sealed face visor. A pack fitted to the rear of the suit held a small cylinder, which contained enough oxygen to sustain him for fifteen minutes. It would be long enough. Next to the body suit was a thick, tube-shaped plastic container. It was no more than eight-inches long and slightly thicker than a cigar tube. Tarrant unscrewed the threaded top and removed it. The inside was filled with a soft foam compound, and a metal shape protruded from the foam.

Tarrant eased it out carefully. When it was completely exposed, he was holding what looked like a silver ballpoint pen, except that one end had a black nylon cap fixed to it. This was the release mechanism. Once he depressed the black cap, there would be a two-minute delay before a steel needle punctured the membrane over the inner seal and released the pressurized virus into the air. There was enough virus in the container to kill at least fifty people. In this instance, Tarrant was after only five. The Armageddon Virus would do its work with deadly, silent efficiency. Colorless and odorless, it would spread quickly and kill with terrifying speed.

Closing the bag, Tarrant left the car. He took his time, making certain no one was patrolling the exterior. Satisfied, he made his decision to move. He checked the automatic pistol holstered on his left hip, butt forward, then pulled the bag close to his body and moved quickly. Once committed, Tarrant went directly for the trees, not pausing until he was able to drop into the cover of the thick grass. It took him no more than five minutes to move through the trees, and then he was crouching on the fringes, with the house no more than twenty feet away.

He eased the pistol from the holster and placed it on the ground beside him. Unzipping the bag, Tarrant removed the protective suit and pulled it on. He sealed the wrists of the suit with wide adhesive tape. He pulled the hood, with its transparent visor over his head and closed the seal between it and the suit. Turning on the oxygen supply, Tarrant felt the cold rush of air as it filled the hood. He began to breathe steadily. Drawing on the close-fitting gloves, he took the plastic container and removed the slender cylinder. He held it in his left hand, picking up the pistol with his right, and moved out of the trees toward the house.

He reached the rear door, pausing to peer through the closest window into the kitchen. It was deserted. Tarrant went up the steps and in through the door, crossing the kitchen and halting by the partially open door that led to the living room. He could hear voices from the room, people speaking to each other in German. Tarrant smiled. The source that had provided the information about the strike team had said there was one woman and four men. Tarrant pressed his foot against the bottom of the door and pushed it open a few more inches, enough so that he could look into the room.

They were all there, still clad in the black outfits they had worn for the raid on Loren Breck's home. The five were armed, wearing shoulder holsters that held autopistols. On the table in the center of the room were a number of Uzi submachine guns.

Tarrant raised his left hand. He put pressure on the black cap at the end of the cylinder and felt the slight tremor as the timer activated. He counted off the seconds in his head, waiting until there were only ten left. Then he moved quickly into the room and slammed the door shut behind him.

He covered the five with the pistol.

"You won't make it," he said as one of the five made a halfhearted move for his holstered gun. Tarrant's voice was muffled by the visor, but his words were understood.

"Who the hell are you?" Theresa Meyer demanded, angry at the way the man had caught them.

Five seconds left.

Tarrant turned to look her in the eyes.

"No time to explain," he said. "Auf Wiedersehen!"

Two seconds.

One.

As he held out the cylinder, pointed in their direction, Tarrant saw the needle impact against the membrane. Almost immediately he heard the pressurized hiss as the cylinder expelled its contents. There was a fine mist that appeared for no more than a fraction of a second. Tarrant tossed the empty cylinder onto the table.

Something had to have warned the five that they were on borrowed time. They broke into action. One of the men reached for the holstered gun, fingers curling around the butt. It was as far as he got. His action was halted as an expression of fear crossed his face. He reached up to touch his skin, rubbing at it, then began to wring his hands together.

Across the room the other members of the group were beginning to react as the Armageddon Virus spread with increasing ferocity.

Breath caught in throats. Eyes widened in sheer terror as they began to experience the contagious effect of the thing they couldn't see or smell.

Tarrant stood back, observing. The expression on his face was one of studied curiosity as he watched the five die. There was no malice in his eyes, simply the eager anticipation of someone on the verge of a new experience, and the lack of feeling was all the more chilling because of that.

When it was all over he took a final look, then turned and made his way out of the house. He returned to the cover of the trees and removed the protective suit, packing it back inside the bag. He retraced his steps to where he had left his car. Placing the bag in the trunk, Tarrant sat inside the car and picked up the mobile phone he had brought with him. He pressed a single button that dialed a preset number.

Mohn answered.

"It's done," Tarrant said.

"Any problems?"

"It went perfectly."

"Good. We're leaving now. When you get back to the city tidy up. Don't leave any loose ends."

"I'll take care of them," Tarrant said.

"We'll see you in a couple of days."

"Okay. I'll make that other call now."

Tarrant broke the connection. He keyed in another number, which would connect him to one of Chicago's news agencies. He would give them the chance to get their exclusive before calling the authorities and breaking the news to them.

One way or another, Chicago was going to have a busy night.

THE FIRST OF THE MEDIA vehicles was approaching the house when the telephone began to ring in the living room. It rang for some time before ceasing. Moments later the door opened and the news team barged in....

11

As the car approached the house that Theresa Meyer and her team had been using, Yakov Katzenelenbogen started to feel uncomfortable. Not because he was a newcomer to the images of sudden death, but because he was troubled by the nature of these particular killings and what they signified.

Katzenelenbogen's memory had begun to stir as he became aware of the slivers of information trickling into Stony Man. At first he had only picked up the odd fragment, but as time passed and the details grew, Katz sensed a familiarity with certain facts. Not wanting to offer any comments until he was on firmer ground, the former head of Phoenix Force gathered copies of all the available information and took it away to study, making his assessment on the data as a whole.

The final piece of the jigsaw puzzle fell into place when Brognola received the photographic evidence of the deaths of Theresa Meyer and her team, sent in courtesy of the FBI.

By that time Katz had more or less made up his mind. The reality of the images confirmed the Israeli's fears. Now he took his conclusions, translated them into hard fact and went to see Hal Brognola.

The big Fed took one look at the expression in

Katz's eyes as he laid out his theory and didn't question him. Within a half hour, Katz was on board one of Stony Man's light aircraft, piloted by Jack Grimaldi.

A call through to Bolan advised him that Katz was on his way. The Executioner, long associated with the tactical adviser, knew there had to be something in the wind if Katz had to see the physical evidence. He also had too much respect for the man to even consider questioning his motives.

Grimaldi put the aircraft down at a local airfield, where an FBI car waited to take Katz on the final leg of his journey. With Grimaldi at his side, the gruff Israeli sat silently in the rear of the speeding vehicle, his mind dwelling on memories he was reluctant to review.

The car drew close to the house, and Katz recognized Bolan's tall figure crossing the neglected yard. The soldier looked tired, but he smiled as he greeted Katz.

"Thanks for the time," he said.

Katz nodded, stretching the kinks out of his body. "I like to keep my hand in. Where are they?"

"Inside," Bolan said, leading the way.

As they crossed the yard, Katz noticed the parked vehicles around the building—local sheriff's department, a couple of highway patrol cruisers, FBI and ambulances.

They entered the house. Bolan led the way through to the living room, standing aside so that Katz could have a clear look at the five bodies.

The moment Katz looked at their distorted, ravaged faces he knew he was looking at the Armageddon Virus.

The ugly memories flooded back in an instant, images of the victims affected by the terrible virus developed by Kurt Mohn.

Katz didn't need a second look. The results of Mohn's virus were totally unique.

"Kurt Mohn," he said. "He's the one you need to look for."

Bolan glanced at him. "Should I know the name?"

"We met Mohn a couple of years ago on a Phoenix Force mission. He was running drugs to help finance his New Order Nazi group, and he had a base in the Amazon. He trained his people there and also had a lab facility where he was developing his Armageddon Virus. He would've used it, too. We took out his people and leveled the place. We assumed Mohn was killed along with his virus. It looks like we got that wrong on both counts. Mohn appears to be alive, and so is the virus.

"The guy is a fanatic, but he's no fool. He was brought up on Nazi ideology. It's his total obsession. He has the will, and he has the financial clout to make things happen. If he's here in the U.S., then we've got problems."

They moved back outside, walking slowly across the yard. Bolan thrust both hands deep into the pockets of his jacket.

"How far would he go to get what he wants, Katz?" he asked.

"Mohn? I'd say as far as it takes. I talked to the man. He'd wipe out half the population of this country to achieve his aims. In our eyes he's crazy. Equally, he's totally dedicated to his cause. In certain quarters he'd be classed as a genius. It just depends where you stand in relation to what he's doing.''

''As far as I can see, the guy's a threat that needs to be neutralized.''

Katz nodded. ''You won't be able to reason with him. Persuasion won't work, nor threats. He can't stop. As long as he's able, he'll keep trying. He has to be eliminated.''

As they walked toward the car, Jack Grimaldi detached himself from the side of the vehicle and hurried to meet them.

''How goes it, Sarge?'' he asked.

''It's going,'' Bolan replied.

''Coming back with us?''

Bolan nodded. ''I'm done here. I need to update and reequip. Just give me a few minutes to tie things up with the FBI agent in charge.''

Stony Man Farm, Virginia

WHEN BOLAN WALKED into the Computer Room he found that Aaron Kurtzman and Carmen Delahunt were the only ones on duty. Kurtzman, with the obligatory mug of steaming coffee in his big fist, swung his wheelchair around and greeted Bolan.

''What have you got for me?'' the soldier asked. He crossed to the coffeemaker and helped himself to a mug.

''All the information we've gathered has been fed into the system,'' Carmen Delahunt said. ''We've cross-referenced it with every source we can think of.''

Kurtzman waved a sheet of paper. ''This came over the fax while you were in the air. The FBI managed to get a couple of reasonable prints off that cylinder left on the table in the house. They came up with a name.''

''Jack Tarrant.'' Delahunt passed across a photo. ''That was taken two years ago during a demonstration by some right-wing group in Chicago. Tarrant has always been mixed up with the white supremacy movement. He's in a partnership with a man named Glenn Sutter. They run a gun club. Not your normal target-practice setup. These people are into serious military weaponry and have a place out in the boondocks where they shoot off everything short of nuclear missiles. FBI sources tell us they've been playing host to Black Dawn for a while now, though they haven't broken any serious laws. It isn't a crime to dress up like the SS and run around shooting guns on private land.''

''The way things are shaping up, I think Black Dawn has moved into the big time,'' Bolan said, glancing up from the photograph.

''We're getting the goods on some serious names,'' Kurtzman told him. ''There's been a lot of movement in and around the right-wing organizations lately. A lot of meetings. The leadership is getting excited about something we can't put our finger on.''

''Could be we have that reason now,'' Bolan said. ''Katz figured out the guy likely to be behind the killing of Theresa Meyer and her people. He thinks it's a German named Kurt Mohn. Phoenix Force came across him in the jungle during a mission a couple of years back. He has a virus that can kill in minutes. Katz took out his organization and figured Mohn was dead. They believed the virus died with him, but it looks like it's surfaced again. It killed Meyer's team, and it could also be the same thing that killed her brother, the guy I found in the basement of the Black Dawn building in Chicago."

"Is that the man who had been feeding us information?" Delahunt asked.

Bolan nodded.

"This the same virus we figure the guy in the burned car had?"

"Asher Kolbe? Yes."

"He's on my list," Kurtzman said. "He's a buddy of the other dead guy, Corbin."

Kurtzman took a long swallow of coffee, then placed his mug on the edge of the computer console.

"Both Corbin and Kolbe had been living in Chicago for almost eight months. Then about four weeks ago they dropped out of sight. But their credit cards didn't. Transactions started showing in New Mexico, and the car they were driving had New Mexico plates."

"Private or rental?" Bolan asked.

"Rental. And before you ask, no, they didn't pay for it themselves. It was charged to a company in New Mexico."

"But they were found in the desert near Las Vegas," Delahunt said.

"Maybe they were on their way to try out the virus in Vegas," Kurtzman replied. "But something went wrong and Kolbe was infected?"

"Likely to be as close as we'll get to the truth," Bolan said. "Corbin burns the car and Kolbe to hide the evidence and kill off the virus."

"So why was Corbin killed?"

The soldier shrugged. "Maybe his people don't

like to leave loose ends. Could be the price of failure. What have you got on this New Mexico company?''

''Still working on that one.''

The door opened and Brognola came in, followed by Katz.

''We need to find out more on Kurt Mohn,'' Bolan said. ''I'd guess he's using a different name.''

''Right now we're bringing in everything we picked up at Loren Breck's office. If he was on the Black Dawn payroll, he could be tied in with this Mohn guy. Could be Breck set up things stateside for Mohn. There has to be something on file somewhere, changed names or not.''

''Katz?'' Bolan asked. ''You're the one with knowledge about Mohn. What does he want?''

''The same thing Hitler wanted—a Nazi world, governed by them and for them. He wants purity and an Aryan society. And I'm taking a guess that he's trying to achieve it through Black Dawn. That's why we've been hearing about this merger with the German Black Dawn. An amalgamation gives them clout here and in Europe. A terror campaign using the Armageddon Virus would be Mohn's way to show he means business. He'll use it to show what he can do and prove that the authorities can't catch him or his people.''

''He hasn't got off to a very good start,'' Kurtzman pointed out.

''That won't stop him,'' Katz said. ''Walk or crawl, Mohn will keep right on with the struggle.''

Brognola peeled the wrapper off a fresh cigar.

''From what we've been able to figure, Black Dawn has pulled out of Chicago. Right now we don't know where they are, so we need to get some intel on them.''

"Give me a location on this gun club run by Tarrant and Sutter,'' Bolan said. "It's as good a place as any to start.''

"In the meantime,'' Brognola said, "we'll work on establishing where Mohn operates from, and what he's calling himself these days.''

Katz leaned forward. "Can I say something?''

Everyone looked his way.

"I've had firsthand experience of Mohn's virus. We've now had evidence of it here in the U.S.A. I don't want to scare you, but this man and his damn virus need to be stopped. And stopped fast. If he plans to use it on targets around the country, and puts those plans into operation, then we're going to have big problems.''

"Katz is right,'' Bolan said. "This has to be dealt with on a top-priority basis. But we also have to keep a security blanket over it. If any more news gets out, we could have mass panic.''

"The news item put out in Chicago caused some panic,'' Brognola said, "but we managed to stop them issuing any more. The last thing we need right now is speculation by the media. They know something is up. They also realize it could be very serious so they're cooperating—for now. I don't expect that to last. So we have to shut Mohn down quickly. Contacting the media was a smart move. It got Black Dawn some publicity. Not much, but it proves Black Dawn isn't just talking. They're showing us they can and will use their power.''

"I'm on my way,'' Bolan said. "Get that information ready for when I leave, Aaron.''

"Will do," Kurtzman said, swinging around to face his monitor screens.

Katz followed Bolan as he left the Computer Room and headed for the armory.

"You need any backup?" the Israeli asked.

"You're already providing that, Katz," Bolan said. "The more of you I have here, the more information I can call on."

"Sounds like a solo run."

"Hard and fast, and no time for prisoners."

Katz knew what he meant.

The Executioner was on a collision course with the enemy, and when they finally met, blood would flow. Anyone who got in Bolan's way would be lucky to survive.

12

Mack Bolan's preference would have been to make a night assault, but time was against him once again, so he went in during daylight.

Black Dawn was in the process of building itself a new, hostile image, but now that the Executioner had dealt himself into the game it had taken a deadly turn. The reason for his presence was plain and simple. The gun club was set for termination, chosen as a start in Bolan's attack on the structure of Black Dawn. He'd send a message to the shadowy figures in the background that no matter how they saw themselves, they had no protection against the Executioner.

Two miles from the highway, in desolate country a three hours' drive from Chicago, the gun club was situated in rugged, undulating terrain. It was a sprawling wooden building that housed offices, firing ranges and an armory. A complete kitchen and dining area had been tacked on to the original building.

Bolan, clad in his blacksuit and armed with a 9 mm Uzi submachine gun in addition to his Beretta and Desert Eagle, lay prone in the sparse grass several yards from the rutted track that served as an access road. The track led to a flattened compound, where a number of vehicles were parked in an untidy clutter in front of the main building. Off the road, trucks stood alongside sleeker cars. Bolan identified two of the parked cars as part of the tail convoy that had followed him from Chicago to Breck's home.

A flagpole in the center of the compound flew a Black Dawn flag.

The organization appeared to be taking things seriously. Bolan had already spotted two armed guards, dressed in black combat gear, patrolling the clubhouse perimeter. They were carrying Uzis.

His solitary vigil had been under way for almost a half hour. The time span didn't worry Bolan. He wanted to be satisfied he had pinned down the guards' patrol sequence, and he was also mapping the layout, pinpointing the various sections of the place. He memorized locations, making sure that he had locked on to any possible black spots. Going in was relatively easy—it was getting out that often betrayed the penetrator.

Finally satisfied, Bolan prepared to make his move. He carried out a final weapons' check, then pushed to his feet cautiously. He had timed his move, knowing that he had almost a full minute before either guard would cross his entry trajectory. Even so, Bolan only just made it before the first guard showed himself.

Bolan completed his run, ducking low and rolling under the first of the 4x4 trucks. He lay motionless as the guard strolled into view and walked by his hiding place.

The guard would reach the far end of his patrol

area and meet his partner. They would spend a brief moment together before retracing their steps.

Bolan had decided to make his next move during the guards' meeting point. He had allowed himself ten seconds to clear the far side of the 4x4, cross the open compound and drop-roll into the crawl space beneath the clubhouse.

That part of his assault went without a hitch. He worked his way beneath the building, moving deep into the shadows to avoid being seen.

As he continued crawling over the dusty earth, Bolan picked up the sounds of occupancy coming through the floorboards—the clatter of boots, the snatches of conversation.

The soldier took a break. It was hot under the building, the trapped air suffocating. He lay on his side, head raised as he picked up the sound of voices again. This time they were distinct, the words low but clear.

"Okay, so we didn't find him. The guy's like a damn shadow. Here, there, gone. Jesus, we can't even get a clear description of him."

"For an excuse, that's crap."

"You hold on there. I'm not making excuses. I'm telling it the way it is. This Belasko is good. Let's fucking admit it. He's walked all over our people every time they've met. Don't blame me, Jack, if the facts give you a hard time. I can admit a guy is good and live with it. If you can't, it's your problem."

"So what are you telling me? You're ready to roll over on this guy?"

"No, that ain't it. You know me better than that, Jack. Tell me one time when I ever quit on a job.

Even thought about quitting. I'll tell you when. Fucking never. So don't give me a hard time, because I don't like it.''

''All right, let's calm down. But how about getting our act together and sorting this out?''

''What's the word from the street?''

''Nothing. Belasko has gone.''

''He showed up at Jensen's, blew away two of our guys, then just disappeared?''

''That's it.''

''I want this bastard dead and buried. I don't care how you do it. Or what it costs. I want to go to New Mexico with Belasko's obituary in my pocket. Understand?''

''Yeah.''

''Then get it done. No more excuses.''

Bolan moved on. He had heard enough.

He rolled out from under the crawl space at the far side of the clubhouse, the Uzi up and tracking. To his left a row of trash cans, overflowing with refuse, stood outside the kitchen door. Steam drifted out through the open door and a nearby window. Bolan could hear a radio playing. Stepping up the wooden steps, he walked to the kitchen door and peered inside.

The cook on duty stood with his back to Bolan. He was dressed in black, his sweaty T-shirt bearing the Black Dawn legend across the back. Around the guy's waist was a web belt supporting a holstered pistol. The cook was hunched over a steaming pot on the stove, stirring it with a ladle while he muttered to himself in a low monotone.

As Bolan prepared to step into the kitchen, he caught movement out the corner of his eye. A pair of black-clad figures came into view armed with M-16s.

Eye contact was established within a heartbeat.

The moment passed, leaving no other option open to Bolan. Caught between a rock and a hard place, the Executioner took the lesser of two evils. He moved into the kitchen.

The cook turned at the sudden movement, his face taut with alarm. He registered Bolan's figure coming at him and made a grab for the pistol holstered on his hip.

The gun didn't even clear the holster's lip.

Bolan stroked the Uzi's trigger and laid a short burst of 9 mm slugs into the cook's body. The bullets chewed at flesh and bone, the impacts spinning the guy off balance. He crashed against the stove, knocking pans to the floor, following them down, the front of his T-shirt splashed with red.

Cutting across the kitchen, Bolan hurried out the far door, pausing only briefly to check the layout. It was the dining area, which contained long wooden trestle tables and benches. The wall to his right was comprised of wide windows looking out across the rugged landscape.

Four men sat at one of the tables. By the time Bolan came through the door, they had been alerted by the gunfire and had snatched up their M-16s.

The Executioner burst through the door, the Uzi up and firing. His first volley took out the closest guy, the 9 mm slugs tearing shreds of bloody flesh from his upper chest. He staggered back, colliding with one of the other Black Dawn terrorists. The man's M-16 fired off a short burst as the guy tried to right himself. A burst from Bolan's Uzi clipped his left side, dumping him facedown across the table. Instead of playing dead, the wounded Nazi tried to come back into the game, pushing himself up off the table, half turning and bringing the rifle with him. Bolan's next salvo ended his life.

Bolan dropped to a crouch, firing the Uzi in a blistering figure eight, catching the two survivors as they raced forward, each pumping random shots from their M-16s. His shots caught the terrorist pair midthigh, and they stumbled, pain etching their faces, one losing his grip on his rifle as he clutched for the edge of a table. The soldier rose to his full height, still firing. This time his raking bursts caught the two men in their chest and neck, slamming them to the floor.

Ejecting the spent magazine, Bolan snapped in a fresh one, cocking the Uzi as he raced through the dining area, aware now that the whole site would be on alert. He had only just reached the long room when he heard a challenging yell from the rear, followed by a barrage of automatic fire from M-16s. The 5.56 mm bullets drilled into the wooden partition wall, tearing ragged holes in the thin boards. Bolan dropped, rolling as he hit the floor, coming up on one knee. He raised his head above the edge of the nearest table and saw the two men he'd spotted outside the kitchen. They had separated and were moving between the tables, closing the gap.

The Executioner gained target acquisition, triggering a burst first at one, then the other. The first gunner went down as a line of holes punched through his chest, crashing to the floor and writhing out his life in agony.

The second guy turned and took a flying leap over

one of the tables, dropping out of sight. Bolan dropped flat himself, picking up the guy's black uniform as he crawled between the table and bench legs. Rolling over a couple of times, the solider waited until the Nazi appeared in a slender opening, then laid a long burst across his opponent's path. A dozen 9 mm slugs struck the terrorist and he flipped over on his back, quietly gurgling on his own blood from a gaping wound in his throat.

On his feet, Bolan went through the door that led outside, cutting along the rear of the building. He spotted a concrete structure that stood on its own, away from the main building. Its steel door stood open. Bolan turned in its direction. At the same moment he reached it, two figures stepped from the open doorway, alerted by the outbreak of gunfire. One of the men gripped a heavy autopistol in his hand, and the moment he saw Bolan's racing figure, he aimed the handgun and opened fire.

The Executioner felt the cut of one slug burn across the surface of his blacksuit, just above his left hip. The touch of the bullet was like a solid blow. It made him catch his breath but didn't deter him from his forward motion. The Uzi crackled, laying slugs into the gunner's lower torso. He stumbled back against the concrete wall, looking down at the holes in his body. Bolan fired again, driving the guy to the ground, then turned his weapon on the second guy as the gunner turned to conceal himself inside the building. The soldier's short burst caught him in the shoulder and the side of his skull. The guy lost coordination, slamming into the wall before crashing facedown over the doorframe, one booted foot jerking in spasm.

Reaching the open door, Bolan peered inside the building. He saw what he'd been expecting—shelf after shelf, rack after rack of weapons and ammunition boxes. He was looking at the Black Dawn arsenal. He didn't hesitate. If he was going to maintain his initial advantage over the Black Dawn terrorists, he needed additional weaponry, and this was the right place to be.

Moving inside the building, the Executioner scanned the racks, locating a box of fragmentation grenades. He dragged the box off the shelf and opened it. The grenades inside were primed and ready for use. Bolan helped himself to half a dozen, dropping them into the pockets of his blacksuit. On another rack he spotted LAW rockets and slung a number over his shoulder by the carrying straps.

Back at the armory door, the soldier saw an armed group of black uniformed men walk around the side of the main building. They hadn't spotted him yet, so he slipped out the open door and doubled around the side of the armory.

A pair of sharp eyes spotted him at the last moment. With the alarm raised Bolan kept on moving, away from the armory and toward the open terrain. Reaching a natural dip in the ground, the soldier unlimbered one of the LAWs. He pulled out the tube extensions, arming the weapon, and laid it on his shoulder. He was taking aim when the first of the armed Nazis came into view by the armory. Bolan sighted down the LAW, then touched the trigger. The launcher gave a throaty groan and released its load.

The fiery trail of the rocket cut through the air and slammed into the concrete wall of the armory.

The initial explosion filled the air with flying debris and curls of smoke. The missile had opened a ragged hole in the wall. The force of the blast knocked two of the advancing terrorists to the ground, and before they could regain their feet, Bolan had launched a second rocket. It streaked through the hole and detonated inside the armory. A ripple of explosions erupted as the blast set off the munitions stored inside the concrete building. The armory vanished in a geyser of fire and smoke, shattered concrete and flying shards of metal. The blast engulfed everything within its fiery radius.

Debris was still falling as Bolan headed out, using the pall of thick smoke to cover him. He began to circle, hoping to close in on the clubhouse again and concentrate his attention on the building.

The drone of a vehicle's engine reached him. Bolan threw a quick glance over his shoulder and saw a 4x4 truck swing around the shattered armory and accelerate in the direction of his former position. Armed figures hung out of the windows, and one man was sprawled on the roof, braced against the luggage rack that ran the length of the vehicle.

The roof rider saw Bolan first and alerted his partners. The off-road vehicle turned sharply, almost dumping the roof man to the ground and charged in their enemy's direction.

The Executioner kept moving at first, wanting to gain a little more distance before he turned and pulled his remaining LAW rocket from his shoulder. As he armed the mobile missile, dropping to one knee, Bolan saw the 4x4 slow and come to a stop. The driver had recognized the threat of the launcher, and he attempted to initiate evasive action. The roof spotter had pushed into a sitting position. He struggled to maintain his balance, the M-16 he carried jammed against his shoulder. He began to fire in Bolan's direction, single shots that raised dusty geysers around the Executioner.

The 4x4 jerked to a shuddering stop as the driver lost control and stalled the vehicle.

Before the vehicle could be moved, Bolan triggered the LAW. The rocket struck midway along the side of the body and the 4x4 blew apart. The added explosion of the fuel tank increased the size of the mushrooming fireball that engulfed the shattered remains of the truck. Somewhere within the fiery mass the shredded bodies of the Black Dawn terrorists met their own personal Armageddon.

Dropping the expended LAW casing, Bolan pushed to his feet and pulled the Uzi back into firing position, striding across the terrain, a tall, black figure bringing chaos and sudden death to the Nazi brotherhood.

Another 4x4 lurched into view. Autofire flew from the open windows, black-clad terrorists laying down streamers of fire that chewed up the earth around Bolan's weaving figure. He presented a hard target and the Black Dawn gunners expended ammunition in vain.

The Executioner dropped to one knee, turning at the waist, and brought up his Uzi. Lining up the sights, he laid a short burst through the windshield of the vehicle. The glass shattered, blowing back into the face of the driver. The terrorist let go of the wheel as a thousand stinging needles burned into his flesh. The 4x4 hit a ridge, the wheels turning sharply, sending the speeding vehicle onto its side.

Two of the window gunners were crushed under the body, while the others struggled to pull themselves clear of the upturned vehicle. They were still attempting to scramble clear when Bolan sprinted past the truck and lobbed a grenade through the shattered windshield. It detonated with a dull thump, filling the interior with flying death, tearing the life out of the panicky survivors.

Trotting down a slope in the direction of the clubhouse, Bolan saw the sparkle of water. A shallow stream wound its way across the flatland at the base of the slope. A line of trees stretched out on the far side of the water. The timber would offer him some cover as he made his approach.

The sounds of pursuit reached Bolan's ears. Lack of discipline in the ranks of the Black Dawn terrorists meant constant noise, which gave the advantage to Bolan. He was aware of Black Dawn's presence and their position at any given time. Equipping themselves with modern weapons didn't reduce their inexperience in combat situations.

The Executioner was in the stream now, pushing for the far side, and the moment he cleared the chilly water he broke for the treeline.

Gunfire flew at his back. Bullets snapped at the Executioner's heels, some passing close to him as he weaved his way toward the trees. He heard slugs hitting the closely spaced trunks. Bark and pale wood splinters filled the air.

Bolan plucked a grenade from his pocket. He caught the pin in his teeth and yanked it free, then half turned to hurl the high explosive back across the stream. He had only taken a half-dozen steps into the tree cover when it detonated. Someone screamed in pain.

He paused long enough to snap in a fresh magazine and prime the Uzi.

The soldier plunged deeper into the timber, knowing that the diversion the grenade had created would be short-lived. Somewhere off to his right he picked up the roar of diesel engines as someone drove a 4x4 truck around the far side of the trees.

The pursuit was heating up. The terrorists were pulling out all the stops. Bolan's intervention had to have upset them more than he had anticipated. Whatever they were up to, they wanted it kept totally secret.

Undergrowth crunched close by. Bolan dropped to a crouch, bringing the submachine gun on-line, eyes peering into the shadows thrown by the timber and foliage. A pair of dark shapes moved in and out of the patches of light, pausing for a moment as they gauged their position. The brief time they were still was enough for the Executioner to squeeze off a volley of 9 mm Parabellum rounds. The motionless figures were thrown to the ground as the slugs burned into their chests.

Staying low, the Executioner pushed on. He needed to clear the far side of the trees before the terrorists surrounded it, trapping him. The 4x4 was joined by a second, moving slowly as it rolled into view. The deep throb of their engines warned Bolan that the net was closing around him. Cutting back and forth, using the shadows to conceal him, the soldier slipped through the trees. With no more than a few feet between him and open ground, Bolan watched the cruising trucks as they prowled the area.

He freed another grenade, popped the pin and waited. As the next 4x4 rolled by, he tossed the bomb beneath it, between the wheels, then turned and dived back into the trees.

The explosion engulfed the truck in a ball of flame.

Bolan skirted the blazing wreck, tracking along the edge of the tree line. He saw one of the other trucks racing in his direction and melted into the shadows again, waiting for it to pass. It skidded to a halt, doors bursting open as its four-man crew scrambled out. They were staring in the direction of the fire-gutted wreck, not one of them paying attention to their assignment.

Bolan had no problems with that. It made his task easier as he leaned out from the shadows and squeezed off a shot from the Uzi. The closest of the terrorists dropped from a 9 mm slug through the back of his head, his partner whirling as he went down. All the guy saw was Bolan's black-clad figure rising from the ground, the Uzi already tracking in. The submachine gun cut loose again, drilling a number of slugs into the guy's skull. He toppled back, sliding along the side of the 4x4's body. Alerted by the activity behind them, the remaining two terrorists moved to intervene. By that time Bolan had ducked behind the truck and opened fire. He raised the weapon and swept the gunners with a sustained burst. They went down hard, sprawling in bloody heaps on the ground.

The Executioner swung into the 4x4, pulling the door shut as he put the truck into gear and jammed his foot on the gas pedal. The idling engine surged, and the heavy vehicle lunged forward. Bolan spun the wheel and brought the truck around, heading back toward the clubhouse.

He still had matters to settle. Black Dawn hadn't seen the last of him yet.

13

Glenn Sutter was almost apoplectic. He could see the gun club being razed to the ground and the Black Dawn members shot to pieces. He watched in amazement as the black-clad stranger scythed through the area with comparative ease, taking out any resistance with ruthless finality.

"Now you can fucking well see what I was telling you. Nothing stops this Belasko."

Jack Tarrant didn't comment. He was staring through the window at the smoking ruins of the armory. Inwardly his mind seethed as he digested the loss of the considerable stock of hardware. The cache had been collected over a period of weeks, the weapons and munitions brought in on a regular basis—bought on the black-market, hijacked from military stores. The weaponry had been a significant donation toward Black Dawn's growing status. Now it was gone, destroyed in a few minutes through the actions of a lone man, who now appeared to be removing every Black Dawn member in sight. Tarrant, who had little time for fools, also had little to offer when it came to acknowledging superior talent. He saw Belasko as a deadly threat and one that needed to be removed as fast as possible.

He snatched up an Uzi, ramming a taped double magazine in place.

"And this bunch is supposed to be Black Dawn's storm troopers? What the hell have you been teaching them, Glenn? Jesus H. Christ, if Erlich could see the way they're performing, he'd go out and help Belasko."

"I didn't choose this bunch," Sutter protested. "Erlich said train them. He forgot to tell me they're retards."

"I don't have time for this," Tarrant growled. "I'm supposed to be leaving for New Mexico tomorrow. If I walk in there and tell them we were retired by one guy, *mein Führer* is going to wet his Aryan Jockey shorts. It isn't going to go down too well with his guests, either. You forgotten who he's entertaining out there?"

"The frigging Japs? No, I haven't forgotten. But I don't give a shit."

Tarrant strode across to the door and yanked it open. He paced the corridor, yelling for everyone to move it.

"Let's go. One man is all you heroes have to handle. One man! Now let's see some goddamn action."

He cleared the corridor, peering through one of the rear windows, and saw a 4x4 truck hurtling down the slope behind the clubhouse. The vehicle was picking up speed, rocking and swaying as it traversed the rough ground. If it kept on its present course, Tarrant realized, it would plow straight into the building.

He didn't have to be told who was behind the wheel of the runaway truck.

BOLAN SAW ARMED MEN hurrying to confront him, weapons raised. The volley of rifle fire was lost in the steadily mounting roar from the truck's engine. Bolan slung the Uzi around his neck by the nylon strap, jerking it so that he would be able to bring it into play without delay. Steering with one hand, he pulled a pair of grenades from his blacksuit pocket and dropped them in his lap.

The driver's-side window chipped as slugs struck it, while others clanged against the bodywork. Something hit the windshield and blew a hole through it, then continued on, wedging in the seat's backrest. Bolan ignored the close shots and held the vehicle on its direct run at the building. He made a calculated guess at the remaining distance.

The clubhouse loomed large, and gunners scattered from the path of the truck. Some didn't make it and were hurled aside by the solid weight of the vehicle, bodies broken and lifeless.

Bolan picked up the grenades and pulled the pins, dropping the high explosives on the floor. He reached for the door handle, yanked the catch and kicked it wide. Turning, he launched himself in a full-length dive and saw the ground hurtle up to meet him.

The 4x4 ran on, swerving slightly as the wheels struck uneven ground. The heavy truck tilted, then righted itself seconds before it tore through the rear wall of the clubhouse and burrowed deep into the building. The truck was still moving when the grenades detonated, adding to the destruction. Flame erupted from the ruptured fuel tank, throwing fire in all directions.

Bolan rolled on impact, absorbing the force of

striking the earth at such a speed. He came to rest in a shifting cloud of dust. Gripping the slung Uzi, he gained his feet. Debris filled the air, blowing out from the gaping hole in the clubhouse wall.

Sensing figures closing in, Bolan turned, the SMG spitting death, ripping holes in the advancing Black Dawn terrorists. Two men went down screaming, clutching the bloody wounds, forgotten weapons dropping to the ground as they died. The Executioner scanned the area, trading shots with a solitary gunner. Slugs flew by his face—close, but not enough to count. Bolan's return fire was less wide of the mark, and his 9 mm bullets cored into the target's chest, spinning him off his feet.

Bolan hit the wall of the clubhouse. Smoke was billowing out of the gaping hole. A black-clad man, clothing ablaze, burst from the gap, arms flailing. He stumbled, then fell to his knees. His pained screams ended when Bolan cut him down with a short burst from his Uzi.

JACK TARRANT STARED in angry disbelief at the shambles around him. The building was filling with acrid smoke from its blazing timbers. Outside, the Black Dawn soldiers were spilling their blood as they put up a lackluster fight against the intruder. The whole damn ship was falling apart before his eyes, and Tarrant was in danger of losing it.

Glenn Sutter had run screaming from the wreckage, his clothes alight.

As Tarrant had watched, his ex-partner had been dropped to the ground by a burst of fire from Belasko.

The man was just outside the window Tarrant had

looked through. Without hesitation he lifted the Uzi, aiming it at the attacker's broad back, and pulled the trigger.

The weapon jammed.

Tarrant stared at it, his fury increasing. A misfire!

He worked the cocking bolt, trying to clear the jam. Movement on the other side of the glass caught his attention, and he saw the enemy vanish from sight.

Tarrant threw the Uzi aside, snatching the SIG-Sauer P-226 pistol from his hip holster. Snapping back the slide, he turned and pushed his way through the tangle of shattered timber, making for the opening in the wall. Belasko's reprieve would be short. He wasn't going to get away free and clear. Not after what he'd done to Black Dawn.

BOLAN HEARD TARRANT'S approach before the Black Dawn enforcer appeared. He burst into sight, armed with a handgun, and triggered a hasty shot the moment he saw Bolan.

The 9 mm slug came closer than Bolan liked. He felt its passing as a hot draft of disturbed air near his face.

Tarrant's eyes registered his annoyance at having missed such an easy target. He put pressure on the trigger again, this time adjusting his aim before he completed the pull.

Bolan had already tracked the Uzi on-line, firing off a short burst. His bullets clawed at Tarrant's gun arm, shattering the bone.

Tarrant's shot went into the sky as his hand was jerked off target by the impact of the Uzi blast. He twisted, his body screaming in protest against the pain of his wounds. His SIG-Sauer had disappeared, slipping out of his numbed fingers. Tarrant clutched at his pulped shoulder, bright blood spurting between his fingers.

On his knees, tears of pain filling his eyes, Tarrant sensed Dolan standing over him.

"So finish it!" Tarrant raged.

"It's over for you, Tarrant," Bolan said. "This place is shut down."

"This is nothing. You won't stop the main attraction. It's going to come, Belasko, and you can't shoot it down."

"The virus? We know about that."

"Know what? That it exists?" Tarrant gave a harsh chuckle. "So does half of Chicago after the news broadcast. The thing you don't know is where and when. It could be anywhere, Belasko. None of you will know until it happens, and by then it'll be too late."

"You'll kill thousands. Just like you killed Theresa Meyer and her team. For what? It isn't going to make the government hand power over to Black Dawn. You don't have a hope of succeeding."

"We'll see. When the dead are starting to mount up, then we'll see." Then Tarrant made a play for his ankle holster, trying to unleather his hideaway gun. But he didn't make it.

As Tarrant raised his head, he saw the black muzzle of Bolan's Uzi. The bright light flashed down the long dark barrel, and then there was only blackness.

Before the fire gained a stronger hold, Bolan hurried through the building. In the main office, at the front of the clubhouse, he found information that detailed the locations of additional arms caches in the Chicago area. Other locations were spread around the country. Black Dawn was on the move. The amounts of weaponry and munitions indicated more than just a simple terrorist campaign. The arms stores were substantial. Enough to equip a powerful force. Bolan gathered the material and took it with him as he left. He had a two-mile hike to get back to his car.

14

Twenty-four hours had passed since his hit on the gun club, and, once again in blacksuit, rearmed and ready for war, Mack Bolan prowled the shadows of Chicago, ready to deal out justice to the followers of Black Dawn.

One of the Black Dawn locations he'd found on the information retrieved from the gun-club files was an industrial estate and a distribution company dealing in magazines and paperback books.

Leaving his car, Bolan had closed in on foot. The distribution company stood at the end of a line of other units, each one surrounded by chain-link fences. Some had security lights throwing harsh illumination across the exterior. Bolan's target was less bright. Only one light was on. The rest stood in shadow, and the setup suited Bolan.

He crouched in the darkness, studying the layout. A number of trucks were parked close to where he was situated. Slinging his sound-suppressed Uzi, Bolan scaled the fence, rolling over the top and dropping to the ground behind the parked trucks. He unslung the Uzi, gliding silently between the parked vehicles, and pausing near the front of the line to check out the building. It housed offices, with the main warehouse section in back. At one end were wide roller doors and a loading bay. A lonely, low-wattage bulb burned over the loading bay, providing enough light for Bolan to pick out the shape of a sentry.

Using the line of trucks as cover, Bolan worked his way to the building's front wall, then crept along until he was adjacent to the loading bay.

He could hear the sentry's breathing, the scrape of a match as the guy lit a cigarette. The smell of tobacco reached Bolan's nostrils. The creak of dry door hinges broke the silence as someone joined the sentry.

"Anything?"

"Phones are still dead."

"You figure they got problems out there?"

"It's not like Tarrant to lose touch."

"With all that's been going on, maybe they got hit out there too."

The second man didn't answer.

"So what are you going to do?"

"Already did it. I called New Mexico and told them."

"And?"

"They'll check it. We hang out here and keep our eyes open."

"Hey, it's time I got relieved. My ass is freezing."

"Okay, okay, I'll send out Mason to take a turn."

The door creaked again, shutting with a tinny bang.

Bolan crouched below the level of the loading bay and moved to the far end, putting him behind the sentry. He located the steps that led up to the top of the ramp and went up on silent feet, peering over the top step. The sentry stood with his back to Bolan, hands shoved deep in the pockets of his pea jacket, shoulders hunched. He carried a stubby Uzi, dangling from his shoulder by a short nylon strap.

Aware that the sentry's replacement could show at any second, Bolan rose to his full height. He came up behind the unsuspecting sentry, looping the Uzi's nylon strap over the guy's head, then back against his exposed throat. Bolan rammed a knee hard into the sentry's spine, increasing the pressure with a sudden pull. The sentry coughed out his cigarette, clawing at the nylon that was grinding into his throat. He stood little chance. Bolan's attack was swift and sure, his technique brutally efficient. The sentry expelled a final shocked gasp. Bolan held a few seconds longer, then sensed the loss of resistance. When he lowered the sentry, the man slumped with the total looseness of death.

Stepping over him, Bolan made for the metal side door. He was almost there when it opened and a man stepped through. The soldier had no time to turn aside.

The newcomer, carrying an Uzi himself, took one look at Bolan and reacted instantly, swinging around his submachine gun to target the Executioner.

Still moving forward, Bolan launched a powerful kick that caught his adversary high in the chest, slamming him back against the shutter door. The door bowed under the weight, then sprang out, pushing the guy away. Off balance, the man found himself stumbling into the muzzle of Bolan's suppressed Uzi. The SMG fired a muffled burst that cut into the guy's chest, blowing out between his shoulders. The terrorist went down with surprise still etched across his face.

Easing open the access door, the Executioner slipped through and broke right, coming up behind a stack of bound magazines. He peered over the top of the stack. The dimly lighted warehouse stretched away from him. Bolan made out lines of shelves holding more magazines and books. To his left was a block of offices and a washroom.

A door opened and a man's head and shoulders leaned out.

"What are you doing out there, Mason? Keep the damn noise down."

When he didn't get a response, the man pulled back through the door. A moment later, armed, he stepped out into the warehouse, two other gunners crowded behind him.

"Artie, go check the lockup."

The man named Artie headed toward the far end of the warehouse. The other men advanced.

Bolan stepped out in front of them, his Uzi raised.

Without pause the Black Dawn terrorists responded in kind, weapons coming up and firing.

The Executioner had the advantage of surprise. It was thin, but it was all he needed. The suppressed Uzi opened up, sending an almost silent stream of 9 mm slugs winging in the direction of the advancing neo-Nazis. They were caught in the middle of the volley, bodies punctured from waist to throat, and they tripped backward under the impacts. Their bleeding bodies slammed against the concrete, twisting and writhing.

Bolan discarded the used magazine, ramming home a fresh one as he trotted along the rows of racks, seeking the third gunner. He spotted him on the far side of the building as the man turned, alerted by the firing.

Unaware of his partners' deaths, Artie began to walk back the way he'd come, then saw Bolan. He didn't stop to open fire. Instead, he dodged out of sight behind a stack of cartons.

The soldier caught his move and did the same, coming to the other side of stacked goods just as Artie reappeared. Bolan triggered the Uzi, laying down a sustained burst, and chunks of pulped paper blew out from the stack. The Executioner ran along the racks and picked up the squeak of shoe leather on concrete, a soft moan of sound. Artie fell into view, stumbling to his knees. His Uzi dropped. The front of his shirt was a glistening mass of red. Bolan's shots had torn the front of his throat out, and red streams of blood were spilling down his chest. He stayed on his knees for a few seconds, then fell facedown on the floor.

Turning back, Bolan checked out the office rooms. They were clear, the only signs of habitation the mugs of coffee on a desk and a still-smoking cigarette. On a shelf, a portable television set was playing an ancient black-and-white movie.

Making his way to the rear of the warehouse where he'd seen Artie, Bolan reached a brick-built block with a steel door. Heavy bolts held the door closed. The soldier slid the bolts free and hauled the heavy door open. It was like looking at a carbon copy of the armory he'd located at the Black Dawn gun club—on a smaller scale, but still holding considerable firepower. Stepping inside, Bolan checked out the mix of weaponry and munitions. He found the blocks of C-4 plastique he was looking for. On another shelf he located timers and detonators.

The Executioner returned to his car and drove away from the area, not even looking back when he heard the distant explosion that destroyed another Black Dawn cache. Bolan had much to achieve in the coming hours. He had to reach and take down two more locations before the leaders of Black Dawn got wind of what he was up to.

SITE TWO HAD A PAIR of guards standing over its arms cache. In appearance they were identical—tall and heavily built. Black garbed, each man sported a crew cut, and tattoos on their brawny arms. They carried Uzi SMGs, holding the weapons with the awkwardness of newcomers to the sophisticated hardware.

It was well past midnight when Bolan completed his approach, crouching in the shadows behind a stack of empty fuel drums filling a corner of the auto wrecker's yard. The site was a graveyard for abandoned vehicles.

The pair of watchers were focusing their attention around the dark workshop. It was a long building, with high metal doors. The Black Dawn hardmen were in a constant state of movement, wandering in and out of the building, as if the responsibility of guarding the weapons was stressing them out.

Bolan was on hand to relieve them of that pressure, and he had no time for a drawn-out confrontation. He waited until one of the men disappeared inside the workshop, then moved up quickly behind the other guy and jabbed the muzzle of his submachine gun into his spine.

PLAY "LUCKY 7" AND GET
THREE FREE GIFTS!

HOW TO PLAY:

1. With a coin, carefully scratch off the silver box at the right. Then check the claim cha to see what we have for you — **FREE BOOKS** and a gift — **ALL YOURS! ALL FREE!**

2. Send back this card and you'll get hot-off-the-press Gold Eagle® books, never befo published! These books have a cover price of $4.99 each, but they are yours to kee absolutely free.

3. There's no catch. You're und no obligation to buy anything. V charge nothing — ZERO — f your first shipment. And you do have to make any minimum numb of purchases — not even one!

4. The fact is thousands of readers enjoy receiving books by mail from the Gold Eag Reader Service™. They like the convenience of home delivery…they like getting the be new novels BEFORE they're available in stores…and they love our discount prices!

5. We hope that after receiving your free books you'll want to remain a subscriber. B the choice is yours — to continue or cancel, any time at all! So why not take us up on c invitation, with no risk of any kind. You'll be glad you did!

YOURS FREE!

PLAY LUCKY 7 FOR THIS EXCITING FREE GIFT!

THIS SURPRISE MYSTERY GIFT COULD BE YOURS FREE WHEN YOU PLAY

LUCKY 7!

"The Uzi," Bolan said and took the weapon as it was passed back to him. He ejected the magazine, then tossed the submachine gun into the darkness. "Inside. You know what I'm looking for. Go."

Bolan jabbed the muzzle into the guy's spine, drawing a subdued gasp. The man had the sense to cooperate, walking ahead of Bolan into the dimly lighted workshop where half-stripped cars and trucks jockeyed for space on the cluttered floor. The warm air was heavy with the odor of oil and diesel fuel.

"Get your buddy out here," Bolan demanded.

The hardman stopped.

"Problem?" the Executioner asked.

"When he sees you, he'll likely start to shoot. I'm not going to take your fucking bullet."

"Your choice. He might shoot you. I will. Now call him."

The guard still hesitated. Bolan could almost hear his brain working overtime. When he reached his decision, he acted on it without wasting another second.

"Hey, Ralph, get out here," he yelled.

Bolan spotted movement inside the office. A shadow spilled across the floor, and Ralph stepped into view.

"What?" he yelled back.

Bolan's hardman turned suddenly, moving quickly despite his size. He leaned away from the soldier, sweeping his right arm around, steel flashing as the switchblade knife in his hand snapped open. He ducked and thrust, the tip of the blade stabbing at Bolan's chest. The Executioner, expecting some kind of move, swept the barrel of the Uzi down, smashing it across the guard's knife arm. The blow deflected the path of the blade, and it burned a thin gash across Bolan's upper arm. Giving a half-angry, half-scared yell, the guard looped his left arm around, the back of his fist clouting Bolan across the side of the head. Bright lights burst in front of the soldier's eyes and he stumbled away from the man.

"Cut the fucker down, Ralph!"

The workshop echoed as Ralph opened up with the Uzi. Slugs filled the air, clanging off metal.

Bolan let himself drop to the floor, rolling until his progress was halted by a massive engine block. He turned around to face Ralph and saw the big man lumbering in his direction, peering into the shadows that partly obscured Bolan.

The Executioner had a clearer view of Ralph. The man was outlined by the light spilling from the office, his bulk offering an easy target. Bolan tilted the Uzi and stroked the trigger, the suppressed SMG spitting a hail of 9 mm projectiles that hammered into Ralph's chest. He staggered, emitting a grunt, and fell off to the side, his own weapon firing into the floor.

Bolan picked up a sound, almost like someone stifling a sob. He pushed to his feet in time to see Ralph's buddy coming at him wielding a long bar of steel. The bar whistled as it swept down at Bolan. He dropped and rolled, hitting the floor hard, the Uzi jarring from his hands. He heard the bar smash against the metal engine block. As he pulled himself upright, his attacker grunted with the strain of lifting the thick bar again, and it caught the light as it sliced the air. Bolan crouched, then launched himself at the guy, slamming his shoulder deep into his adversary's thick gut. The big man toppled backward, tripping and falling with a muttered curse, then scrambled upright again with surprising speed, and lunged at Bolan.

The steel bar swept down, this time missing Bolan by only a fraction. The Executioner twisted aside, clawing the Beretta from its shoulder rig, pulling his hand across his body and triggering a 3-round burst into the Black Dawn hardman. The slugs pushed the guy off his feet, and he fell hard, still holding the bar.

Bolan located his Uzi. He was breathing hard, his body bruised from the encounter. He began a search of the workshop and found the arms cache after pushing through the clutter at the rear of the building.

He was on his way to his third location when the explosion lit up the night sky.

FORTY MINUTES LATER he was closing in on his final strike of the night.

This time it was different—they were waiting for him.

15

The airfield was small, an independent outfit that served local businesses. Storage warehouses and administration lined the perimeter, and at that early hour there was little activity.

Bolan approached along the service road, driving slowly as he checked out the immediate area. Even before he reached the official entrance to the field, he sensed something odd about the setup. Driving by, eyes kept straight ahead, he noticed the extra attention the security guard in the hut paid him. Glancing in his rearview mirror, he saw the guy lift a cellular phone and speak into it urgently, his head swiveling to watch Bolan's progress along the service road.

The sense of unease grew, and was suddenly manifested in the shape of a dark sedan that pulled out of the shadows behind him. Before it pulled fully onto the road, the car came to a jerking halt, as if someone had ordered the driver to stop. It was too late. Bolan had spotted the car. He touched the gas pedal, and the rental car surged forward.

The tail car accelerated, falling in behind Bolan. A second car rolled out of the darkness ahead of him, sweeping across the road in an attempt to block him. The soldier held his course, maintaining his speed, watching the maneuver of the car. At the last moment he hauled the wheel to the left, sweeping around the rear of the blocking car. Bolan felt the side of his vehicle scrape the rear of the other car. He stamped down on the gas pedal, pushing his car away from the roadblock, the tires burning against the tarmac.

The enemy cut loose, the steady stream of bullets cutting the air, missing Bolan's vehicle by yards. A quick glance in his mirror showed both cars swinging into pursuit. As they drew beside each other they accelerated with surprising speed, closing the gap. Bolan's standard rental picked up speed with agonizing slowness. He reached across and drew the Uzi closer. It was fully loaded, with a double magazine in place.

A bend in the road appeared suddenly. Bolan eased up on the wheel and the rental slid into the curve with a squeal of tires. He felt the rear end going and concentrated on bringing it back under control. The car slid over the edge, bouncing as the wheels hit gravel. Bolan could hear stones rattling against the underbody. He hauled on the wheel, fighting the pull of the car to stay on the road's edge.

Out the corner of his eye he saw one of the chase cars drawing alongside. The soldier glanced to his left and saw a gunner leaning out of an open window, the dark outline of a submachine gun resting on the windowframe.

Stamping on the brake, Bolan risked being pulled off the road. His car skidded, raising a cloud of dust and stones as it lurched sideways, away from the chase car. Even over the slither of tires and roar of engines Bolan heard the vicious chatter of gunfire.

He gripped the wheel, guiding the rental car into a half circle, feeling the wheels bounce and grab at the ground.

Bolan hammered the brake pedal to the floor, bringing the car to a shuddering stop. He yanked on the door, grabbed the Uzi and rolled out of the car. He scrambled to his feet, turning into the glare of headlights belonging to the second car as it curved toward him. He laid a burst of suppressed autofire into the passenger seat, hearing glass shatter and the yells of injured men. The car turned, going into a broadside slide. Bolan realized he was directly in its path and hurled himself clear. He landed in the grass at the side of the road, and heard the solid thump of the chase car crunching into his rental.

Tires smoked against the tarmac as the lead chase car came to a halt. Doors burst open and a quartet of armed figures scrambled out. They sprinted toward Bolan's direction, shouting commands. They fanned out around the stationary chase car and Bolan's rental.

The Executioner targeted one moving figure and laid down a scything burst, knocking the running man off his feet. He crashed to the tarmac with a hoarse cry, the back of his skull impacting with a sodden thud.

Turning, Bolan caught another man sweeping around the front of the rental. The gunner opened up the moment he spotted the soldier's crouching form. His shots thudded into the bodywork of the cars.

Returning fire, the Executioner changed position, circling around the three cars, trading shots with the Black Dawn gunners. He moved constantly, staying in shadows as much as possible, his blacksuit enabling him to remain almost invisible. Down on one knee he exchanged magazines, snapping the second of his double load into place, then took out two of the opposition as they moved into the glare of taillights on the stalled chase car. His shots tore into their bodies, driving them back against the trunk of the car. Slugs cored in the bodywork and one punctured the fuel tank. Leaking gasoline spilled onto the road. The spillage went unnoticed as the firefight continued, with Bolan delivering sudden death to the terrorist group at an alarming rate.

Gasoline vapor ignited with unexpected ferocity. Triggered by stray sparks from bullets striking metal, the rush of flame spread across the tarmac, tracing the fingers of fuel. The glare illuminated the combat zone, giving away locations.

Bolan hit the ground, stretching prone across the road, the Uzi pushed out in front of him.

The Black Dawn gunners, caught out in the open, were slower to react and Bolan's searching automatic fire took out one man, wrenching his life from his body as 9 mm slugs burned into his flesh. The survivors scattered, one of them taking cover at the front of the car that had collided with Bolan's. His decision was less than wise. The burning gas had crept back beneath the leaking car, as well as away from it, and without warning the punctured tank exploded. The pair of vehicles were engulfed in a writhing ball of flame, bodywork bursting open, filling the air with shredded metal. The guy crouching in the vicinity was reduced to a howling scarecrow wrapped in flames. The horror of his fate froze the remaining Black Dawn gunners as their gaze was drawn to the grisly sight.

Bolan didn't allow himself to be distracted. He pushed up off the ground, the muzzle of his Uzi tracking the figures outlined by the flames. He stroked the trigger and took them out with a stitching figure eight, dropping them where they stood.

The soldier lowered the submachine gun. He skirted the blazing wrecks, checking out the downed terrorists. Behind him he heard the rising wail of a siren as a security prowl car moved across the airfield toward the main gate. Once it left the airfield, it would be at the site of the firefight within seconds. Bolan didn't have time to explain things to suspicious security cops. He made his way to where the undamaged chase car stood some yards down the road and slid in behind the wheel. The engine was still running. Bolan leaned on the gas pedal and cruised away from the scene with the lights off until he was well clear. Then he hit the gas pedal and left the area. Twice he had to pull into the shadows as police cars raced by him, lights flashing and sirens blaring. Taking the long route, away from the main roads, Bolan worked his way back into the city. He had things to do that wouldn't wait.

And the first was to contact Ryan Kelly.

"YOU DIDN'T NEED to do this in person," Bolan said as Kelly eased himself stiffly into the passenger seat.

The cop grinned. He closed the door then settled himself in the seat. He took a couple of deep breaths, pressing his hand against his bandaged side.

"Give me a minute," he said.

Bolan rolled the car out of the hospital parking

lot and back onto the street, driving across town toward the police department.

"Been having a busy time?" Kelly asked, eyeing Bolan's disheveled appearance.

"Kind of," the soldier answered. He gave the cop a brief rundown of the events that had taken place.

"Soon as we get to the office I'll get a car sent out to the airfield and have them secure this arms stash."

"I need to get the details of the other caches through to my people," Bolan said. "If Black Dawn has got the word around, they might try to move the stuff. We need to get to them first."

"It'll be good to get back to the office," Kelly said. "I was starting to climb the walls of that damned hospital. They were going to let me out in a couple of days. I just made the decision for them."

"I'm grateful for the help, Kelly."

"No problem."

The department was quiet. Kelly led the way to his office, fending off the greetings of his fellow officers with short nods. Bolan received interested stares as he followed the cop. Closing the office door, Kelly indicated the fax machine, then moved to pick up a phone. Bolan took the folded paper he'd picked up at the gun club and tapped in the Stony Man number. He fed the sheet into the machine, then picked up a phone and called the Farm.

"I'm back at Kelly's office," he said when Brognola came on the line.

"How's he doing?"

"He just broke out of hospital to give me some cover and provide a base for a while."

"What's going on down there?" Brognola demanded. "Feedback suggests World War III."

"Slight exaggeration," Bolan said. "Data coming through needs immediate action. Locations of Black Dawn arms caches. The local ones are out of the game. They've got their hands on some heavy gear—LAWs, explosives, timers, small arms and ammunition. Don't hold back on this, because these people are serious."

"I take your point, Striker."

"Got any info for me?"

"Looks like Kurt Mohn is calling himself Konrad Meinster these days. Same initials, different names. The Bear managed to get the background on this New Mexico company that keeps cropping up. It's called the Sand Bluff Software Company, set up near a small town called Mason's Crossing. It's owned by Meinster. The Bear worked back from that and pulled his passport details. The photo on the application was identified by Katz as being Kurt Mohn."

"Anything else?"

"The gun club was part of the Meinster group. It was taken over about six months back. So was the Black Dawn Chicago HQ. I'm guessing that when we do some digging the locations you've just sent will all have some kind of link back to the Nazi leader. Loren Breck's name kept popping up too. Seems he arranged all the deals and acquisitions for Meinster. By the way, we've also extended our checks as far as Germany and it seems that Herr Meinster has his fingers in a few pies over there. The Black Dawn organization owes quite a lot to his philanthropic gestures."

"I'll bet. I need a cover for Mason's Crossing. Clothing. Credentials."

"Local law involvement?"

"No. If Meinster can buy a cop here in Chicago, he can do it in New Mexico. I'll play solo."

"Striker, we got medical reports from Atlanta. They completed autopsies on Theresa Meyer's team. It gave them more than they got from the body in the car from Vegas."

"Was Katz right?"

Brognola sighed. "He was right. According to the CDC, the bodies had been attacked by a virus that worked so damn fast they never stood a chance. This bug goes right in for the kill. It multiplies so fast it overwhelms every organ in the body, turning them into jelly."

"So even if you had people standing by with an antidote, they wouldn't have time to administer it?"

"Not a chance, Striker. If you get hit by this virus, you don't walk away."

"Then we have to stop Meinster before he gets this stuff on the streets."

"So we can't risk pulling in the other agencies. This has to be done fast."

"Get back to me," Bolan said and cut the connection.

Kelly had also completed his call.

Bolan filled the cop in with the information Brognola had given him.

"God help us."

"In this case we help ourselves," Bolan said.

"I just got information on a local snitch getting himself wasted. He had a talent for finding people. Even out of town."

"Theresa Meyer's safehouse?"

"Even something like that."

"And?"

"He was Stan Jensen's main man."

"Black Dawn uses him to point the finger for Tarrant so he can deliver the virus, then kills him to shut him up."

"Fits their profile."

Bolan closed his eyes. He was starting to feel the weariness drifting over him now that he was inactive. His battered body was telling him he needed to rest. Kelly read his mind and went to the door, calling in a young rookie.

"Eddie, a favor? We need hot coffee and something to eat." Kelly pulled money from his pocket and handed it to the cop.

"Any feedback from Breck's office?" Bolan asked.

"I heard that the secretary Jensen whacked is going to be okay. Bad headache and mad as hell. She's already identified Jensen as having been a regular visitor to the office. He sometimes had a guy with him who turns out to be the late Jack Tarrant. We have people going through Breck's files, and it looks like they'll be coming up with similar information as your people—Breck doing deals for a guy named Meinster, here and in New Mexico. There's a lot more they haven't broken down yet. There was a house on lease to Konrad Meinster. We sent a team out to look it over, but the place was deserted. It had been used recently. Up to a couple of days ago. According to a local lace-curtain snooper, the tenants just up and left. Apparently they had a regular stream of visitors. When she was asked for any descriptions, she did give one that might have been Meinster.''

''Could be he decided to relocate in New Mexico because things were heating up for him here.''

''The way New Mexico keeps cropping up I'd hazard a guess it's going to be your next stop.''

Bolan nodded.

Kelly's telephone rang. Picking it up, the cop listened to the caller for a while, then interrupted.

''Calm down, Benny. Don't go figuring every shadow has a hired gun waiting just for you. No, I didn't say that. Sure I believe you. Look, I'll meet with you. Pick you up and get you out the city for a while. No, I won't be on my own. I'm having a hard time standing up never mind driving. We'll be with you in half an hour. Just stay put, Benny.''

Kelly put the phone down and caught Bolan's eye.

''That was Benny Hon. A snitch I've used for years. He's been checking out some of Jensen's former buddies, seeing if he can pick up on anything we might have missed.''

''And?'' Bolan asked, sensing there was more to come.

''He was trailing some heavies when they took out Jensen's snitch. Trouble was they spotted him. Now he's too scared to show his face. He wants my help to get him out the city. I said I'd go and bring him in.''

''And you want a driver?''

The cop smiled. ''You heard.''

''Couldn't help. Let's go find your boy.''

Before they left the department, Kelly managed to find a leather jacket for Bolan to pull over his blacksuit. On their way out Kelly asked for the food and drink order to be put on hold until they got back.

With Bolan behind the wheel, they drove across town in the direction of Soldier Field, where Benny Hon was waiting.

Kelly fell silent after a while, and his lack of conversation drew Bolan's attention.

"Something troubling you?"

Kelly started to shake his head, then looked across at Bolan.

"Benny sounded odd," he said.

"Could be the guy was scared."

"Benny Hon is one tough Chinese cookie," Kelly said. Then he chuckled. "I'm starting to sound like an old woman. Forget it, Belasko. The guy has a right to be jittery."

Following Kelly's directions, Bolan drove to the spot Benny Hon had said he would be waiting. The soldier pulled the car to a stop, and they sat peering out across the stadium frontage. Kelly glanced at his watch, then opened his door.

"I see him," he said.

Bolan followed his gaze and saw a slim, short man moving out of the deep shadow cast by the stadium. As Kelly stepped from the car, the man began to move in their direction.

"Don't get careless," Bolan warned.

"Just watch my back," the cop said.

"You got it."

The Executioner watched Kelly cross to meet Hon. As the two men closed the gap between them, Bolan leaned forward, easing the Beretta from its holster, then opened the car door.

His instincts were urging him to follow Kelly and

put a stop to the meet. There was something wrong with the setup. Kelly's own misgivings were crowding Bolan's thoughts. The cop's unease at Hon's attitude on the phone should've been enough to warn them both off. Maybe they were running on less than one-hundred-percent efficiency. Too much had happened in too short a time, and even the most dedicated soldier lost the edge when fatigue began to creep in.

A hint of movement in the deep shadows behind Kelly drew Bolan's attention. He focused on the spot, narrowing the block of shadow until he was able to make out the shape of a man shouldering a stubby automatic rifle. A thin shaft of light played along the barrel as the weapon tracked Kelly's walk toward Benny Hon.

Bolan exited the car, gripping the Beretta in both hands. He swung the pistol in the sniper's direction and brought it on target.

"Kelly! Hit the dirt!"

The Executioner stroked the Beretta's trigger, the pistol coughing out a 3-round burst.

The sniper's black shape jerked to one side, then he crashed to the ground.

Bolan covered the ground in long strides, checking out the angles.

Ahead of him Kelly lay prone, pulling out his service automatic.

The slight figure of Benny Hon paused in midstride, and his wailing yell cut across the shadowed area.

"They made me do it..."

"Goddammit, Benny, get down," Kelly roared.

Gunfire shattered the night, and a stream of bullets cut into Benny Hon's exposed back. Dark gouts erupted from his chest as he was pitched facedown on the ground.

The Beretta chugged 3-round bursts in the direction of the gunner. The hard crack of Kelly's autopistol added its punch, slamming shot after shot at the sniper.

The squeak of shoe leather reached Bolan's ears. He heard the snap of a bolt being pulled back and turned in that direction. A hard-faced gunner, wielding an Uzi, stood with legs braced apart as he fought to bring his weapon on target.

Bolan raised the 93-R and triggered a burst that clawed away the gunner's throat. A second trio of rounds cored into the guy's chest.

The Executioner ejected the spent magazine and snapped in a fresh one.

"Kelly!"

"I'm okay," the cop yelled back. He had pushed to his feet and ran to join Bolan.

"Bastards!" he said.

They retreated, aware of the silence that had fallen around them.

The sound of a car engine gunning to life reached their ears. Headlights tunneled through the darkness as the vehicle swept toward them.

Automatic fire exploded with sudden ferocity. The ground erupted from the impacts of slugs as the car loomed large.

Bolan and Kelly ducked below the window level of their vehicle as the attack car drew alongside, bullets still hammering at them. Glass shattered, slugs pounding the bodywork. The enemy car had almost come to a standstill.

Bolan crouch-walked to the rear of his vehicle, working his way around the trunk, then leaned out and triggered tribursts at the slow-moving attack car. His shots blew out the windshield, filling the interior with flying glass and 9 mm projectiles.

Taking his cue from the Executioner, Kelly maneuvered to the rear of the vehicle and began to trigger shots through the rear and side windows. He kept up his barrage until the 92-F's slide locked back on an empty breech. Kelly ejected the magazine and snapped in a reload. He cocked the weapon and trained it on the attack car. There was no more resistance from the vehicle. It had rolled to a stop, the engine stalling as the driver's dead foot slipped from the pedal. A rear door swung open, and a bloody figure slithered out and fell to the ground.

Bolan, his Beretta still held in a two-handed grip, checked out the interior of the vehicle. He moved from man to man, refusing to relax his stance until he had satisfied himself there was no chance of further aggression.

Kelly took a look at Benny Hon. When he returned to Bolan, the look on his face answered any question he might have been asked.

"In the back," the cop said bitterly. "Poor son of a bitch never stood a chance."

"They don't give up easily," Bolan stated. "Looks like there's only one way to deal with Black Dawn. And it isn't by talking to them."

Kelly raised his head as the distant wail of sirens cut the night air.

"At least we won't have to walk home," he said wearily. Leaning against the side of the car, he caught Bolan's gaze. "When you get to New Mexico, Belasko, don't waste time. Just take these mothers down. Send them where they belong—under the damn ground."

16

Mason's Crossing, New Mexico

Deputy Chet Raven watched the lone passenger step down from the noon train and cross to the ticket office. He spent a couple of minutes in conversation with Gus Quigley, then picked up his single piece of luggage and began to walk toward town. Raven picked him up in the rearview mirror. The newcomer reached the motel and stepped inside.

Leaning forward, Raven fired up the Cherokee's engine and cruised along to the depot, where he parked and climbed out. The heat struck the lean, young deputy the moment he exited the air-conditioned comfort of the vehicle. Closing the door, he crossed to the ticket office.

Quigley saw him coming and leaned across to open the door. Raven stepped inside, removing his wide-brimmed hat and running a brown hand through his thick black hair.

"He asked if there was any place in town where he could rent a 4x4," Quigley reported, a faint grin on his thin lips. He was an old man, his life spent in Mason's Crossing working for the railroad company, and talking to visitors meant a break in the tedium. "Told him he needed to see Ed Berrinson down at the gas station."

Raven nodded. He crossed to the water cooler and helped himself to a paper cupful.

"Say what he's here for?"

"Maybe," Quigly said slyly. "Thought that was what they paid you for, Chief."

Raven grinned. "I told you not to call me that. One day my Indian side is going to go crazy, and I'll come after your scalp."

Quigley stroked a hand over his balding head.

"Be a lot of fuss over nothing," he said.

"I'll find something to cut off."

Quigley's cackle followed the deputy as he wandered back outside, returning to the patrol vehicle. The truck was layered in pale dust, a mixture of sand and salt from the flats that bordered the isolated town. The County Sheriff emblem on the doors was almost obscured. Raven decided that the first chance he got he would have the Cherokee washed before Sheriff Rone got a look at it. Rone would bawl him out if he was in a picky mood. And lately Rone seemed to be in a bad mood every other day.

Raven swung the Cherokee around and drove down the street, heading for the diner that stood just on the edge of town. Half a dozen cars were already lined up outside the diner. The deputy spotted one that belonged to the Sand Bluff Software Company. That would probably mean the German guy would be in the place. Raven checked his rising anger. It didn't mean the German would be hanging around Jenny again, but Raven wouldn't have taken odds on that one.

He pushed open the door and stepped inside the

diner, feeling the cool air from the conditioner wrap around him. The first thing he saw was the tall, blond German guy called Klaus Erlich. He was seated on a stool at the far end of the counter, talking animatedly to Jenny. She was being polite, as usual, like she always was with customers, but Raven could see the look in her eyes.

He walked to the counter, exchanging greetings with people he knew, and caught Jenny's eye. She smiled when she saw him. Erlich didn't, as he realized Raven had shown up. He continued to dominate Jenny's time.

"Coffee, please," Raven said.

Jenny said something to Erlich and moved in Raven's direction. She picked up the coffeepot and a fresh mug. As she placed the mug in front of him and started to pour, Raven could see the flush of color in her cheeks.

"Hey, you okay?" he asked.

She nodded, a little too quickly for Raven. He felt his anger rise again, checking it because he knew that was just what Erlich wanted—a confrontation so he could justify the trouble that would follow. And Raven, on duty as a local law officer, wasn't permitted the luxury of personal emotions clouding his judgment.

"He bothering you?"

Jenny looked at him, taking a deep breath. She reached out to touch his hand where it lay on the counter.

"I can handle it, Chet," she said softly. "Part of the job. You should know that by now."

"Not the way this guy is coming on to you."

"You can't arrest him for looking at me." Jenny

grinned. "I'm supposed to be the best-looking girl around here, you know. That's why the local deputy is going to marry me. Right?"

"Which is why I don't like you having to put up with that creep."

"Deputy Raven, I appreciate your concern. But I'm a big girl, and I've been known to handle the odd nuisance customer."

She was referring to the time she had actually dealt with a particularly offensive drunk trying to paw her. After every means of friendly persuasion, Jenny had objected to the drunk's hand on her thigh. She had laid him out with a single blow from a cast-iron frying pan and had then gone on to serve a stunned row of customers.

"Honey, this guy isn't a drunken truck driver. There's something about him I don't like. He worries me. I reckon he could turn nasty."

"Hey, I still keep that frying pan handy."

Raven picked up his coffee.

"You want something to eat?" Jenny asked, changing the subject. She felt better now that Chet was in the diner.

"I'll have one of those sandwiches you make so good."

"Smooth talker. No wonder I fell for you with lines like that."

Raven watched her walk away. As she passed Erlich, the German said something to her, but Jenny ignored him and vanished into the kitchen. Erlich turned to glare in Raven's direction, only to find the deputy smiling at him. Fishing change from his pocket, Erlich dropped it on the counter, then turned and stalked out of the diner.

Swinging on his stool, Raven watched the tall man climb into his car and pull away with tires raising a cloud of thick dust. When Erlich hit the road, the squeal of rubber on pavement could clearly be heard.

Raven drank his coffee, his mind still on Erlich and also on the newcomer who had arrived on the noon train.

THE MOTEL WAS BASIC but comfortable. At first glance it looked just like the motels portrayed in countless Western movies. Inside, the decor and amenities were slightly more twentieth century. The rooms had color television—but without access to the porno channels—and the bathrooms were fully equipped with showers.

Mack Bolan dropped his heavy carryall on the bed, crossing to stare out the window.

The town certainly lived up to its frontier image with its single main street. Trucks were parked at the curb instead of horses, and heat haze shimmered along the black ribbon of road. The air was still, barely a hint of a breeze. In the far distance a range of low mountains nudged the cloudless sky.

Bolan's trip in from Chicago had given him time to read and analyze the printouts of information Stony Man had collated. They had prepared a full dissertation on all the known facts surrounding Black Dawn and Kurt Mohn, a.k.a. Konrad Meinster. Most of it Bolan already had firsthand experience of.

Brognola, by whatever feat of magic, had even obtained an acknowledgment that Theresa Meyer's team had been operating in the U.S. on a strictly unofficial basis. Their deaths had come as a shock to the German administration, who felt some obligation to cooperate with the big Fed, and faxed Brognola background material on Black Dawn's activities in Germany. This highlighted the organization's attempts at moving into mainstream politics and its subsequent humiliation at the polls. From this came the sinister hints that Black Dawn might be in the process of mounting some kind of terror campaign designed to force the issue of its very existence.

Konrad Meinster had emerged as the new driving force behind the organization. His second in command was one Klaus Erlich, a younger man with high ambitions. Brognola had included identifying photographs with his reports.

Bolan's main area of interest centered around Meinster's business in New Mexico, and Mason's Crossing in particular. He had stepped in and bought up the Sand Bluff Software Company, a bankrupt facility that had been the brainchild of a local-boy-made-good. The software company had employed people from the surrounding area and had been seen as a means of reviving the fortunes of Mason's Crossing. The motive had been fine, but Frank Keno, the man behind the company, had run out of luck and money before he was able to fulfill his ambitions. He'd left town just ahead of his creditors. The company—fourteen months old—had been shut down and had remained that way until the appearance of Konrad Meinster. He had bought the company, reemployed the previous staff and started trading again. Things appeared to be looking up for Mason's Crossing.

Bolan's information gave him only the bare bones of the story. He was going to have to find out the rest for himself now that he had arrived in town.

Once he had settled in, he left the motel and made his way down the street to the gas station owned by Ed Berrinson. Bolan's casual stroll allowed him to evaluate the town. He had checked out the place before leaving Stony Man Farm. Mason's Crossing was a long-established town. It had been laid out in the mid 1800s, by a far-sighted man named Jonathon Mason. He had seen the coming of the railroad and had bought up the land on either side of the proposed track. Mason's Crossing, as the place became known, had a checkered life. The town grew to a certain size, then seemed to stagnate because although the railroad came, the boom didn't. The town became a supply point for ranches in the area and the nearby Army garrison. But there were never any high times involving Mason's Crossing. It just existed, a small town set down in the rugged landscape, just far enough to be isolated but not far enough from civilization to be totally removed from the mainstream. Over the years the pace of life in the Crossing never varied.

Reaching the gas station, Bolan sought out Berrinson. He was a lean, sandy-haired character, with a slow manner and an easy way about him. He showed Bolan the vehicles he had for rent, and the Executioner chose a dark blue Ford 4x4. It had the look of a vehicle that had already known a tough life and would go virtually anywhere.

"She in good condition?" Bolan asked.

Berrinson shielded his eyes from the hot glare of the sun.

"Take you anywhere," he said. "More important, she'll bring you back."

Bolan examined the truck, casting a critical eye over the engine. There were no telltale leaks of oil, no rust stains showing on the radiator. Hoses were in good condition, with no cracks. These would be important considerations when driving in the arid terrain around Mason's Crossing.

Ed Berrinson watched the soldier with a thin smile on his lips. He leaned against the front fender, wiping his hands on a rag.

"Not the first time you done this," he observed.

"Don't want to have to call you out on recovery," Bolan said. "Bet you charge a heap."

The old man laughed, a hearty sound. "You'll do, Mr. Rawson, you'll do."

Bolan dropped the hood and fished out his wallet.

"I'll take her for a couple of days. If I need her longer, I'll come in and see you."

"Come on inside and we'll fix you up."

He followed Berrinson to the office. It was stuffy inside, despite the fan that was whirring sluggishly. The walls were decorated with overlapping posters and charts. Berrinson obviously didn't believe in removing old paperwork. He simply stuck the new ones over the top.

"You mind if I get nosey?" Berrinson asked, shuffling papers around on the desk.

"Not particularly," Bolan said, leaning against the wall, his eyes studying the street. He was watching a black-and-white Cherokee 4x4 cruising along the street, dust misting the air behind it. The local law was taking an interest in him, as well.

"So what brings you to Mason's Crossing?"

Bolan skimmed a layer of bills off the roll in his wallet, holding them out to Berrinson.

"Work," he said. "I'm scouting locations for a film company. They're planning a big action-adventure movie and need the kind of locations you have around here. I look over locations, take photographs, go back to Los Angeles and give my report."

Berrinson chewed over the explanation.

"Anything in particular you looking for?"

"Some high ground. Desert landscape. Dramatic rock formations. Things that look good in a wide-screen movie."

The old man pulled a folded map out of a drawer and spread it across the top of the desk.

"This is the town. You need to go north. Here. You got a wide creek that runs through this big gorge. Plenty of high rock faces. Timber along the bottoms. Even a waterfall once you get deep inside."

Bolan traced a line across the map, tapping a point that lay to the southwest.

"Flatland there? Maybe desert?"

Berrinson nodded. "Damn right. Dry as they come. Sand dunes. Some salt flats. Ain't much out there except rattlers and the odd lizard."

"Looks like I'm going to have my work cut out for me."

"Some advice? Make sure you got reserve gas and water on board. Take a bedroll and some food with you in case you go too far to get back by dark. Once you get off-road, it can get pretty hairy driving in the dark."

"Thanks." Bolan studied the map again. He

pointed to a location. "Sand Bluff. That sounds interesting. Anything there?"

"That's owned by a feller called Konrad Meinster. German guy. He bought up a closed-out business and got her on the go again. Employs folk from town."

"What do they do?"

"High tech," Berrinson said, smiling. "Computer software. Hey, I know it sounds out of place, but what the hell. It pays wages. And Meinster has it running like clockwork. His own trucks take the stuff out to a shipping depot in Las Cruces. Other stuff goes out on the freight train. Never had too much time for Germans, but you have to hand it to Meinster. He's got everything running smooth as you like. Can't fault the guy there."

"I guess not," Bolan said. He paid Berrinson the going rate and took the paperwork the man passed him.

"When you planning to go out?"

"I'll make a start in the morning."

The old man followed him outside. Bolan climbed in and started the Ford. The engine purred to life smoothly.

"Told you." Berrinson grinned. "You call by in the morning and we'll make sure you have a full tank and spare gas and water."

Bolan shook the man's hand.

"I'm obliged."

The soldier rolled the truck onto the street and drove back toward the motel. He watched in the rearview mirror and couldn't help smiling when he saw the black-and-white Cherokee pull into the gas station. A lean, black-haired young man in a tan uniform climbed out and went to talk to Berrinson.

"HIS NAME'S BILL RAWSON," Berrinson said. He straightened up after scooping a bottle of Coca-Cola soft drink from the freezer that stood just outside the office. Easing off the cap, he took a long swallow.

"Who we talking about, Ed?" Raven asked innocently.

"The feller you been sitting and watching. He works for a movie company in Los Angeles. He's out here looking for locations for a film. That's why he hired the truck. So's he can go looking. You want a Coke?"

Raven nodded. "Hell, why not. I don't have anything too pressing now you've done my job for me."

The deputy took the bottle Berrinson handed him and washed away some of the dryness in his throat. He wished it could wash away some of the doubt that lingered in his mind where Mr. Bill Rawson was concerned. Admittedly, he didn't know what movie location scouts looked like, but he was sure as hell they didn't handle themselves the way Rawson did. He was too confident, too aware of his surroundings. The man was in Mason's Crossing looking for something. Chet Raven didn't believe it was movie locations.

Sand Bluff

"SIT DOWN, KLAUS," Mohn said as Erlich entered the office.

The newcomer closed the door and chose a chair that kept him out of the bright sun shining through the window behind Mohn's desk. He could sense there was something wrong. His superior's tone was low, calm, very controlled, which usually meant he was about to deliver bad news.

"Events are happening almost too fast for me to take them in, Klaus."

"Have I done something wrong?"

"Not so much done something wrong as done things badly, Klaus."

The telephone rang. Mohn snatched it up and listened, then snapped out a curt reply and replaced the receiver.

"Our Japanese colleagues are becoming impatient so I'll have to cut our meeting short."

Erlich began to stand up, but Mohn waved him back with a flick of his hand.

"I said cut it short, not cancel it," he said. "While you've been in town, reports have come in from Chicago. The gun club has been hit, and we suffered heavy casualties. Both Tarrant and Sutter are dead. The club burned to the ground and the arms cache was destroyed. Following that, two of the other Chicago area caches were also destroyed and our people with them. The third cache has since been raided by the authorities."

Erlich stared at Mohn as if he had spelled out the end of the world. He had no words to say.

"To give our people in Chicago credit, they attempted to assassinate the policeman, Kelly, the one who shot Jensen. It was purely a precautionary measure in case he had gained information when he searched Breck's office. They used one of Kelly's trusted informers to lure him into the open. However, our friend Belasko turned up with the cop and they wiped out our people, save one who managed to avoid the firefight. He got through to me and relayed the news.''

''Does that mean the authorities are on to us?'' Erlich asked.

Mohn smiled. ''I don't think so. If they had enough evidence, I think we would be surrounded by now. I believe they are still feeling their way. A little unsure. Which is why our Mr. Belasko is in Mason's Crossing.''

''Are you certain?''

''The clerk at the motel is being paid very well to inform me of any strangers who show up. He called some time ago to tell me about a man who had just arrived. He's calling himself Bill Rawson. His description fits Belasko exactly. He says he's a scout for a film company searching for locations, and he has hired a Ford 4x4 truck. No doubt he'll be out our way to look us over.''

''He won't get close enough,'' Erlich snapped.

''Caution, Klaus. The last thing we do is kill him under suspicious circumstances. Use your head. We need a few more days to complete production of the virus. Killing Belasko, or Rawson as he is now calling himself, and having the police crawling all over us isn't a wise strategy.''

''If we leave him alone...''

''Listen, Klaus. We'll get rid of him, but make it look like an accident. Let him drive away from town, somewhere you can stop him. Then push his damned truck over a cliff, down a ravine. With him inside it. No bullet holes, Klaus. Keep us out of it.''

Erlich nodded. ''I'll see to it.'' He paused. ''What about Chicago?''

Mohn shrugged. "What is done is done. It's a great inconvenience. However, it had already served its purpose. We were going to move everything out here eventually. The city would've been nothing more than a staging post, a distribution center for that part of the country. Here we can regroup, gather more people. We have our contacts and they're no farther away than a telephone call. One good thing about this country is that it has excellent communications. Yes, we have lost a battle, but the war is only just beginning. We'll have our day. Once we have the virus in quantity, we can show the Americans what real fear is like. The lost weapons can be replaced. So, in fact, can the people. Don't forget, Klaus, we are in America. The land of plenty."

17

At seven-thirty the next morning, Mack Bolan entered the diner and sat at the counter. A few customers were already eating. The aroma of coffee and
fried bacon assailed Bolan's nostrils, and he realized
just how hungry he was. The previous evening he
had sent out for coffee and sandwiches, which he
had eaten in his room as he went over the Stony
Man reports. After a good night's sleep he was re-
freshed but hungry.

The dark-haired woman behind the counter
brought a big smile and a pot of fresh coffee. As
she filled the pot mug in front of Bolan, her frank
gaze drew his attention.

"Sorry," she apologized. "Bad fault of mine. I
just like to check out newcomers."

Bolan smiled. "Check all you want. Then could
you bring me bacon, a couple of eggs and some
toast?"

She nodded. "My name is Jenny Cade. How do
you like your eggs?"

"Facing the sun," Bolan said.

She laughed. "You got it."

He watched her go. She was young, pretty and
had the confidence of someone with her life ahead
of her. Bolan's thoughts, prompted by the young

woman's fresh appeal, turned to the reason he was in Mason's Crossing. He was acutely aware that she was one of the reasons why he had to end Black Dawn's plans to let loose the Armageddon Virus. For a brief moment he imagined her young face swollen and bloated by the virus, just as Theresa Meyer's and her brother's had been following their exposure to the terrible weapon. Bolan could not— would not—allow the man now known as Konrad Meinster to unleash his weapon of terror on an unsuspecting America. Or elsewhere.

The soldier was well into his breakfast, with Cade refilling his mug, when the diner's door opened and the deputy came in. The moment she saw him her eyes lit up, and the expression on her face told Bolan how it was between her and the young cop.

"Hi," she said, leaning over to kiss him on the cheek.

The customers let out a ragged chorus of good-natured approval. Chet Raven grinned self-consciously, while Cade beamed at the encouragement.

Raven took the empty stool next to Bolan. He glanced at the Executioner and nodded.

"Morning."

"Bill Rawson," Bolan said. "Arrived yesterday."

"Chet Raven, deputy sheriff. I saw you get off the train and go to the motel."

Bolan picked up his coffee. "Checked me out with Ed Berrinson, as well."

"You don't miss much," Raven said. He held out a mug for Jenny to fill.

"You were doing your job. I was getting ready for mine."

"I hear you work for a movie company in Los Angeles."

"Bet you know what I'm going to be doing."

"Checking out possible locations for a movie." The deputy took a swallow of coffee. "Like you say, I'm just doing my job."

"Sometimes you take it too seriously," Cade said over the counter. "Don't embarrass the man, Chet. He'll think we're a suspicious bunch in Mason's Crossing."

"I don't mind," Bolan told her. "The deputy has every right to check out strangers in town. A man needs to know who his friends are."

"Or his enemies," Raven added.

"Or his enemies," Bolan agreed. "Know your enemy and you already have an advantage over him."

The young woman rolled her eyes to the ceiling. "Why don't you two go outside and do some male bonding. I'll check this coffee. I must be making it too strong because everyone is turning all macho."

Bolan grinned as she turned away to serve someone at the far end of the counter.

"She gets a little outspoken sometimes," Raven explained.

"Don't apologize. You've got a great girl there, Deputy. You hang on to her."

"I aim to." Raven swiveled on his stool. "So tell me, Bill Rawson, just what else are you here for?"

"Already told you. Location spotting. Take a few photographs of likely places, make some notes, then back to L.A. and the smog."

Raven studied him for a moment, his dark eyes looking beyond the outer skin. After a while he slowly shook his head and went back to his coffee.

"Damned if I can figure it," he muttered.

"Something bothering you, Deputy Raven?" Bolan asked flatly.

"Tell the truth, yeah. You bother me, Mr. Rawson. I can't put my finger on it, but there's something that doesn't sit square."

Bolan placed money on the counter, drained his coffee and stood.

"Thanks for the breakfast, Jenny." He paused at the cop's elbow. "When you decide what's bugging you, look me up, Deputy Raven. I'll be interested to hear what it is."

The Executioner walked out of the diner and climbed into the Ford. He drove down to Berrinson's gas station and loaded up the extra gas and water. The old man handed him a bottle he'd filled with fresh drinking water.

"Recall what I said yesterday?"

Bolan placed the water bottle on the passenger seat.

"Take things easy. If I get caught at night, find a safe place and park until morning."

"She can get a touch cold out there after sundown. You got night gear?"

"Bedroll and blankets. Picked them up at the store before I turned in last night. I got a small gas stove and coffee makings, too."

"I guess you done this before?"

"Some."

"You take care now."

Bolan climbed into the Ford and drove out of Mason's Crossing. He followed the route he had worked out on his area map the night before. It took him off the main highway after a few miles and onto a narrower, dirt trail that wound its way through dusty hills, climbing gradually. After an hour, Bolan was able to park on the side of the trail and look back over the way he had come. Below him he could see Mason's Crossing, the straggly lines of the town with the steel rails running alongside glinting in the sun. He could see thin columns of smoke rising from the chimneys.

He drove on, aware of the time restriction placed on his shoulders by the criteria of the mission. If Black Dawn was planning a terror campaign using the Armageddon Virus, it would be soon. The onus would be on Mohn to develop his virus and distribute it quickly to his followers now that it was obvious that his cover had been blown.

The Executioner was on his own for this mission. It had been decided a lone hand was the only way to play it, which was why Hal Brognola had manipulated a complete security shutdown over the whole affair. The big Fed, in consultation with the President, had agreed with the assessment Katz and Bolan had put forward.

As far as Bolan was concerned, it was the way he always worked. Only this time he was getting the green light because Mohn was so unstable. An alternative plan wasn't possible. Swift action. No prisoners. No mercy.

The Ford pushed deeper into the desolate terrain. Bolan drove in a random pattern, stopping when he saw a likely place to take photographs, then moving on again. His intention was to circle the Sand Bluff area, placing himself in such a position so he could check the place over. If anyone was watching him, his driving pattern would hopefully give them the impression he was on some innocent pursuit.

Mason's Crossing, 9:35 a.m.

KLAUS ERLICH SAT behind the wheel of his car, fingers gripping the wheel tightly. He was parked outside the motel, having just been inside to inquire about the man calling himself Bill Rawson. The desk clerk had told him that Rawson had just left, saying he was going for breakfast before heading out of town.

Snatching up the car phone, Erlich punched the number of the facility and waited. When the phone was answered he asked to be put through to Meinster's office.

"Well?" Mohn asked.

"He has already left."

"An early riser," the Nazi leader taunted. "A man after my own heart. I'll send out the reception committee. You make your way out to meet them. Keep in touch by phone, and Jardine can guide you in intercepting them. Then you can take command. I don't want to waste any more time. I'm going to be in conference with our Japanese comrades for most of the day."

The connection was broken, leaving Erlich holding a silent phone. He slammed it back in its cradle, muttering in anger. He was about to drive away when he saw Jenny Cade crossing the street. She stopped to wave as Chet Raven drew up beside her.

She climbed into the Cherokee beside him, and they sat talking.

Erlich started the car and dropped it into gear. He swung it around and drove out of town, the tires screeching on the pavement.

RAVEN WATCHED Erlich's car speed out of town even as Jenny was still telling what she had overheard while in the motel lobby.

"I was at the newsstand, kind of out of sight, I guess. Erlich came in like his pants were on fire and went straight to the desk to talk to Henry. I wasn't paying too much attention at first. Then I heard Henry telling Erlich that Bill Rawson had left early, that he was driving up-country to do some scouting for locations. Erlich got real agitated then. He told Henry to keep his eyes and ears open and to call if he picked up anything. Just before he left I heard him say something about Meinster wanting results and Henry being paid well. I waited for a while after Erlich left and Henry went through to the office. Then I left."

"Looks like I was right about Rawson," Raven said. He wasn't bragging. Simply stating the fact. "He's no scout for the damn movies."

"Never mind about Rawson's so-called job. What about Erlich? Why is he so interested in the man's movements? And just what is Henry being paid to supply to them?"

"Information I suppose," Raven said. "There's something going on up at Sand Bluff, and I don't mean the computer business."

"Drugs? What?"

Raven shrugged. "Right now, I don't know. But

I mean to find out. Bill Rawson is involved though I don't think he's on Meinster's team. Not the way they're checking on him.''

He started the Cherokee.

"I'll see you later, Jenny."

The woman leaned back in the seat, arms folded, staring straight ahead.

"Hey!" Raven said.

"If you think I'm staying out of this now, you must be crazy. I want to know what's going on, Chet.''

Raven rolled the Jeep away from the curb, muttering to himself. He knew better than to argue with Jenny Cade once she put her foot down.

Staying well back, Raven trailed Klaus Erlich's car. He knew the country far better than the German, so he was able to think ahead and guess which way the man would be going. He was also able to take shortcuts and hidden trails that few others knew existed.

They drove for almost two hours. At the end of that time they were well away from the regular road.

It was Cade who spotted Erlich's abandoned car, which had been parked off the trail, in thick brush. Raven drew alongside and sat for a while, checking the area. It took him some time, but he finally picked up the faint dust trails in the distant air. A little later he saw the slow-moving trio of 4x4s far ahead, climbing into the hills.

"I see them," she said when he pointed in the direction of the distant vehicles.

Raven stepped out of the Cherokee, his handgun drawn. He walked around the car, peering inside, then returned to check out the tire tracks in the dust.

"They came in from that direction," he said. "Met up with Erlich, then moved on."

"Chet, I'm starting to get a bad feeling about this. I think they're looking for Bill Rawson but not to invite him to dinner."

The deputy returned to the Jeep and climbed in. "Let's try to find him first."

"Do you think Rawson will be trying to get close to Sand Bluff?" Cade asked.

"It's the way I read it. If I wanted to take a look without being seen, I'd take to the high country. A man with good binoculars would be able to get a clear view of the bluff."

"The problem is, Erlich will probably see it that way too."

Sand Bluff Area

Bolan had gotten to within a few miles of Sand Bluff when he realized he wasn't alone.

He'd been driving in the general direction of the bluff, but still a good distance from the facility when he caught the flash of something reflecting in the rearview mirror.

He kept driving, giving no indication he had seen anything. But as he drove, he scanned all the mirrors on the Ford. It took almost five minutes before he picked up a sighting, a dark-colored 4x4 easing into a thicket on a rise behind him. Keeping his fix on the point, Bolan spotted a second vehicle edging in close to the first one.

They were tailing him, keeping him under observation.

For what?

They might decide to remove him—but not by shooting him. They'd need to make it look like an accident. If they had been intending to take him out by sniper fire, it could have been achieved at any time. The fact that they were closing in without resorting to any firepower suggested they were going to use other methods.

Bolan edged the Ford across an open stretch of hillside, turning the vehicle around a high boulder. Ahead of him the terrain flattened out for some considerable distance. He wished for less of an open space.

Behind him the roar of an engine split the air. The Executioner glanced over his shoulder and saw one of the trucks bouncing down the slope in his direction. They had to have decided to make this their killing ground.

Bolan reached out and drew his backpack to him. He slid his arms through the straps and cinched the waist belt. Wearing the pack made sitting uncomfortable, but he didn't want to have to evacuate the Ford without it. Under the light windbreaker he wore the Beretta in a shoulder rig. The .44 Magnum Desert Eagle was holstered on his hip.

Dropping the Ford into gear, Bolan hit the gas pedal and sent it surging forward. He wasn't going to sit this out and wait for them to come. Until he knew just how big a force he was up against, a shooting match wasn't advisable.

The Ford rolled across the uneven terrain, raising a thick cloud of dust in its wake. The landscape didn't lend itself to high-speed driving, and the 4x4 wasn't designed for it, either. Bolan was going to have to make the best of what he had.

He hit the flat close to fifty. The suspension sent hard vibrations through the vehicle, and though he had power steering the soldier found he needed both hands to keep the wheel from spinning out of control.

A glance in his mirror showed the chase truck stuck to his tail, coming up fast. It appeared to be equipped with a better engine than Bolan's vehicle. He responded by working up through the gears, ignoring his own safety as he pushed the truck to even greater speed.

The level area fell behind him, and the soldier felt the truck hit rough ground. He saw the terrain ahead start to rise. There was a high bluff forming, with the rough trail curving around its base. Bolan went for it, as it was the only avenue open to him.

The Executioner yanked the wheel to the right, around the base of the bluff. The Ford's front end lifted as he hit an unseen object. He hung on to the wheel, guiding the bouncing vehicle between the rocks and fallen timbers that littered the way. More than once he felt the raking drag of rocks scraping the bodywork.

Throwing a swift glance in the mirror, he caught a glimpse of the chase vehicle as it maintained its relentless pursuit, hanging on to his tail. Whoever was handling the truck knew his business, and he wasn't about to be left behind.

The trail ahead of Bolan began to narrow as he approached a high rock slope on the right. The left-hand side of the trail dropped away in a treacherous shale slope that ended in a brush-choked ravine some sixty feet below.

The chase truck surged forward, closing with a sudden burst of speed. Bolan floored the pedal, urging every ounce of acceleration from his vehicle. He gained a little, but the chase truck seemed to have a greater reserve of power, looming large in the rear-view mirror.

It rammed the rear of Bolan's vehicle and almost threw him off his seat.

The Ford slithered offtrack while Bolan fought to stay on the road. Thick dust was thrown up by the spinning wheels, and stones showered over the edge of the trail.

Bolan corrected the slide. The trail curved toward the slope and he aimed for that, hoping to keep the Ford away from the edge.

Behind him the chase truck accelerated again, slamming hard into Bolan's bumper a second time.

They were trying to force him off the trail and down the almost sheer slope. They were attempting to manufacture an accident, to make his intended death appear the result of bad driving.

The 4x4 shuddered violently as the chase truck rammed him again. The Ford's rear end banged into the base of the slope, shredding away crumbling sandstone. A heavy cloud of dust rose in Bolan's wake, completely hiding the chase truck. The Executioner took the chance and stepped on the gas, trying to gain some distance. He was driving by sheer determination, hauling the wheel around to keep the careening 4x4 from going over the edge, his speed increasing with every passing second.

By the time the chase truck reappeared, the soldier was yards away, pushing his own vehicle forward with total disregard to the driving conditions.

The trail curved away in a right-hand bend. Bolan eased the wheel and brought the truck into the bend. As he cleared the curve, he saw a second 4x4 ahead of him. This one was angled across the trail, blocking his way.

Bolan leaned forward and freed the passenger door, stamping on the brake. The action locked the

Ford's wheels and threw it into a headlong skid, thick clouds of loose dust billowing around it.

Seconds later the 4x4 slammed into the truck planted across the trail. The impact pushed the stalled vehicle to one side and sent the gunmen scattering for cover. The rear wheels went over the edge and it rolled, raising dust as it slid down the slope. Bolan's Ford, brought to a near-standstill, rolled after it.

As the front of the 4x4 bounced over the road's edge, Bolan pushed the open passenger door wider and launched himself through it. He hit the slope feet below the trail. His hands searched for a grip, slipped, then found purchase. As the falling trucks crashed downslope, with the sound of tortured metal, Bolan dragged himself into the cover of the overhanging trail, pressing into the hollow provided by the crumbling ledge. The cascading clouds of thick dust enveloped him, covering him from head to foot. It blended him into the contours of slope as he hugged the surface.

The final, rending crash of tumbling metal was followed by the dull thud of gasoline igniting, as spilled fuel swallowed hungry sparks from some electrical circuit. The flames reached halfway up the slope, turning quickly into a smothering screen of dark smoke.

The chase truck came to a stop, doors clicking open. Bolan could hear pounding boots as the passengers met with the man from the other truck. They moved to the edge of the trail, peering into the fiery ravine.

"Fried the son of a bitch."

"Any volunteers to go get his fucking scalp?"

"Let's go. It's time we were out of here."

The subdued grumble of the idling truck engine rose as it pulled away. Bolan remained where he was until the silence surrounded him. He moved carefully, digging in his heels and easing himself over the edge of the trail, rolling his aching body onto solid ground. Turning his head, he stared into the ravine. Smoke still trailed up from the tangled wrecks.

The Executioner got to his feet and headed back along the trail until he cleared the high slope. He pushed into the untidy sprawl of rock and brush, finding a spot where he could see without being seen.

Inactivity increased his awareness of his bodily aches. He had taken a hard fall when he had exited the 4x4. His body was starting to react to the impact, and Bolan knew he should be on the move. Staying still was only going to stiffen his aching joints.

He checked his watch. At least another hour remained before the light started to fade.

The day was still hot. Bolan could've done with a drink, but his water bottle had gone into the ravine with the Ford. He didn't dwell on the loss. There was no point. Instead, he concentrated on what lay ahead of him—a trek through the darkness until he reached Sand Bluff.

"BASTARDS! THEY RAN HIM off the trail and straight over the edge."

Chet Raven lowered the binoculars, staring across the hood of the Cherokee at his girlfriend.

"I wouldn't have believed it if I hadn't seen it."

The explosion from the ruptured tanks of the

wrecked trucks reached them. Raven put the glasses to his eyes and scanned the distant scene, watching the flame and smoke rising into the air. After a few moments the deputy turned away.

"Chet, what's going on?"

"I don't know, but I'm going to find out."

"I don't think so," a familiar voice interrupted.

Raven turned and looked into the muzzle of a heavy automatic pistol.

"You had to interfere, Mr. Policeman. Just when we had everything sorted out," Klaus Erlich said.

Raven dropped his hand to his holstered gun. A faint smile edged Erlich's mouth. He swung the pistol in a short arc, clouting the cop across the side of the head. The powerful blow spun the deputy off balance. He slumped over the hood of the Cherokee, blood streaming down the side of his face. Then he slid down to the ground, kneeling in the dust, blood dripping from his face.

Jenny Cade moved quickly round to Raven's side. She ignored Erlich as he reached over to remove Raven's handgun and tuck it behind his belt.

"Move away from him," Erlich snapped, his patience evaporating as he saw the situation slipping from his control.

The woman looked up at him from where she crouched beside Raven's slumped form.

"Or what? You'll shoot me? I believe you would, too. It's probably the only way you can act like a man."

Her words angered Erlich and he lunged at her, the gun raised to hit her.

The woman sprang upright suddenly, her right hand sweeping in at Erlich's face. It was only in the last moment that he saw the fist-sized chunk of rock in her hand. Then it struck him full in the face. Erlich heard his nose snap and felt blood gush down his chin. He staggered back, dazed, pain flaring. Cade hit him again and again, each blow measured and hard. He stumbled over something and went to his knees. In his pain and confusion he thrust out his gun hand and fired. The sound of the shot was loud. The bullet went wide. Another blow, this time to the side of his skull, dropped him to his knees. He felt a hand yank the gun from his belt. Panicked, he tried to rise.

Chet Raven, half risen, saw Cade grab his weapon back from Erlich. He pushed away from the Cherokee, lurching unsteadily in her direction as he saw the German, his face and head bloody, push to his feet and turn toward her.

Without thought Raven made a grab for her, reaching for the gun, his fingers closing over the weapon.

Erlich wiped the blood from his eyes on his sleeve. He made out the figures of Jenny Cade and the deputy, and brought the handgun around to line them up.

Raven pushed Cade aside and heard the startled cry that burst from her lips. Then he sensed Erlich's presence. He looked in the man's direction and saw the raised handgun.

The deputy's own weapon rose at his bidding and he pulled the trigger. Erlich's gun fired in the same instant, the two shots blending into one.

Raven felt something burn across the flesh of his left hip. The impact swung him around and banged him against the side of the Cherokee. He didn't see his own slug core deep into Erlich's chest, kicking the man off his feet. Erlich landed on his back, his gun hand flying open, the pistol slipping from his grasp. Pain flared briefly, expanding so rapidly that Erlich had no time to register it. The light of day caved in on itself and a darkness of great intensity swallowed him, shutting out every other sense.

Raven felt a gentle hand on his shoulder.

"Chet?"

He turned to stare into Cade's concerned face. She helped him to his feet.

"I'm okay," he said, then added, "Erlich!"

"He's down, and I think he's dead," she said. "Now keep still while I get the emergency kit and see to that wound."

Raven admitted to himself he was feeling a little light-headed. And sick. He had never shot a man before, let alone actually hit one. The thought he might have killed Erlich scared him. Not from any queasiness, more from a sense of responsibility. It was no easy thing accepting that he might have taken another man's life.

He crossed to where Erlich lay. Bending over him, the deputy checked for signs of a pulse. There was nothing.

"Oh, Jesus," Raven said softly. He sat beside the body. That was when he realized he was still holding the pistol.

"Hey," she said, "if you hadn't done it, we'd both be dead now."

"We're not, but he is," Raven said. "And I did it."

"I can't say I know how you're feeling," Cade said as she pulled his shirt away from the bloody gash in his flesh, "but I sure as hell won't be losing any sleep over what's happened. Chet, what were you supposed to do? Let him kill us to avoid a guilty conscience?"

"Easy for you to say," Raven said sharply, then let out a groan as she applied a pressure pad to his wound. "Hey, not so rough."

"Then quit being a martyr, Chet. What if Erlich's buddies might still be around and heard the shooting? Let's get out of here and find a place to hide until we decide what to do."

Raven knew she was talking sense. As soon as she had finished bandaging the gash in his hip, he pushed to his feet. As an afterthought he reached out and picked up the gun Erlich had dropped. He had a feeling he might need the additional firepower.

KLAUS ERLICH'S PARTNERS hadn't heard the shooting. They had been inside their truck, moving away from the scene of the accident when the distant gunfire erupted, and the roar of the 4x4's revving engine blanked out the shots.

Someone else did hear, though, someone closer to the source of the shooting.

Mack Bolan.

He turned, trying to locate the sounds, then began to cut across country to check out the incident.

Within a few minutes he picked up the sound of an idling engine. He fisted the Desert Eagle, moving into the cover of a dusty thicket. The black-and-white Cherokee patrol vehicle came into view, and Bolan recognized Chet Raven behind the wheel. He showed himself, and the deputy brought the Jeep to a stop.

He stepped out of the vehicle, Cade close behind. Bolan confronted the deputy.

"Raven, I have a feeling we need to talk."

19

Jardine could tell that Mohn was annoyed at his intrusion but he held his ground.

"I hope you have something important to tell me," the German snapped as he closed the door to the conference room, shutting off the curious stares of the Japanese clustered around the table.

"We dealt with Belasko," Jardine explained, "and you won't find a bullet hole in him."

"But?" Mohn asked, knowing that good news always came with a price attached.

"Erlich is dead too."

For a moment the expression in Mohn's eyes said it all. He regained his composure within a few seconds.

"How did it happen?"

"Erlich met up with us on the trail. We took off after Belasko and picked him up. When we started closing in, Erlich spotted that young deputy from the Crossing. Raven was tailing us. Klaus took one of the trucks and said he'd deal with him. The way he talked it was like he had some personal score to settle."

"Damn him," Mohn said. "It was the woman, the one who worked in the diner. I heard Klaus talking about her more than once."

"Yeah? So we go after Belasko and do the business. Used one of our trucks to block the trail and forced him over the edge. When we were done, we all piled in the truck and headed back. We figured to run into Erlich. Except all we found was his truck where he'd left it. When we found him, he was dead. He'd taken a beating around the head, then a slug in the chest. We picked up his truck and headed back."

Mohn stared out the window, his shoulders slumping for a time.

"I figured you'd want to know what happened," Jardine said to break the silence.

"Yes."

Mohn's shoulders stiffened as he turned and faced Jardine.

"It might be that Belasko and Raven weren't working together. If Belasko had alerted others, I would have expected more than just a local deputy in the area. That could work in our favor."

"Raven is a persistent bastard. He'll still be out there, most likely heading this way."

"Be ready for him then, Jardine. Make sure everyone is ready. This time there's no retreat. We have nowhere else to go. From now we're on full alert. Black Dawn stands and fights."

"Erlich is dead," Jardine pointed out. "Who passes on your orders now?"

The Nazi leader smiled. "Are you telling me you never wished you had his job, Jardine?"

"Hell no."

"Then give my orders and make everyone realize the position we are in."

WHEN MOHN STEPPED back into the room, he felt every pair of eyes on him. He returned to his seat at the table and picked up the paper he had been reading before the interruption.

"As I was saying, gentlemen, the first consignment of the virus will be brought into Kobe docks on board a freighter out of San Francisco. The arrangements have all been made. The ship belongs to one of the companies under my control, so there's no problem with departure dates. It leaves when I say it leaves."

One of the Japanese men leaned forward.

"You have no concerns?" he asked.

The question was polite enough, but Mohn sensed the man had more on his mind than a delicate query.

"Nothing my people can't deal with."

"Should we consider bringing our departure forward?"

"That, Murakawa, I'll leave you to decide. But there are still details to be settled before you leave."

Seated across from Murakawa was a lean, hardeyed younger man. He glanced at his superior, then turned to Mohn.

"We're aware of the problems you've been having," he said without the usual deference of the Japanese to protocol. His name was Osugi, and Mohn had him down as the new breed of Japanese hardliner. He wore his aggressiveness like a badge. "Has it followed you here? We came to strengthen our alliance with Black Dawn, not to become caught up in local problems."

"Osugi!"

Murakawa half rose from his seat, his usually bland features dark with rage.

"You forget we're guests here. Have you learned nothing but contempt for our traditions? To insult our host is to insult me. As long as I'm leader of Crimson Shadow, we'll observe protocol. Your private thoughts remain private."

Murakawa broke into his own language, the harsh words striking at Osugi with a force that made him shrink back, eyes lowered.

"I must apologize," the older man said. "Osugi has much to learn. As with many of the younger generation, he has allowed himself to adopt Western attitudes while losing sight of his own heritage."

Mohn acknowledged the apology with a slight inclination of his head. He didn't want to antagonize Osugi further. The younger man had a quick temper, and his impetuous character had already shown itself on more than one occasion during the Japanese delegation's visit to the facility. His questions were always asked within a cynical frame, as if he were trying to catch Mohn, or his people, off guard. The Nazi leader had quickly taken a dislike to Osugi, but he was also aware that the man was on his way up within the Crimson Shadow group. Osugi, if he survived, would possibly have great influence. Mohn, with future alliances in mind, held his tongue.

"Perhaps this would be a favorable time to take a short break," he suggested, standing. "If you would retire to the next room, you'll find refreshments waiting for you. We'll resume in thirty minutes."

The Japanese filed out silently, as if they were making an apology for the mere act of moving. It was only when the door closed behind them that

Mohn realized he wasn't alone. Glancing up, he saw that Murakawa was still in his seat.

"May I ask a question, Herr Meinster?"

"Of course."

"Osugi did raise a point of interest that prompts me to go a step farther. He mentioned your problems in Chicago. I don't intend to make an issue of that, because it is strictly your own affair. However, my own curiosity makes me ask why you chose America as your base of operations. Why not your own country?"

"Germany is too small, too rigid in its attitudes. It also has a history of controlling those who choose extremes of resistance to the elected party in government. It would've been harder for me to operate over there. The needs of Black Dawn, both here and in Germany, required that I be able to complete my development of the Armageddon Virus without too much interference. America allowed me that freedom. It's so large, so diverse that I was able to set up my organization with comparative ease."

"Forgive me if I say that you don't seem to have had quite the freedom you expected."

Mohn smiled. "True, my friend. I won't deny that. Nor will I excuse it as bad luck. The Americans aren't as naive as we sometimes believe. They were offered assistance by a German national who had penetrated our organization, and though we did catch the informer and dealt with him, it appears he had already given the Americans information that enabled them to move against us. So I decided that we pull back and strengthen our position here in order to complete the final production of the virus. Once we have that in container form, it will be distributed and we'll abandon this facility and move to the next phase of the campaign. Which brings us back to what we have been discussing. The shipment of the virus that will be sent to Crimson Shadow by sea for your collection at Kobe docks.''

Murakawa considered the explanation.

''Can I also add,'' Mohn said, ''that another consideration of basing myself here in America was the proximity to the Pacific territories and Crimson Shadow especially.''

''We are grateful you have extended the hand of friendship toward us. The mutual advantages we'll both receive from this cooperation will profit our movements. Our aims are to create a state of chaos within our country, and to show that the authorities are helpless against something like your virus.''

''Murakawa, how much of a threat is Osugi?''

The Japanese took a slow, deep breath.

''He desires my position greatly. If the opportunity arose, he would strike without hesitation. However, he's without significant support at the present time. If he attempted to kill me—and succeeded—his own life would be forfeit. I expect this situation to change in the future. Osugi is extremely ambitious. If he's able to control his temper and bide his time, then I might have to consider him as an adversary one day. I look forward to that. It'll be an interesting confrontation.''

''I sometimes wonder if the greater enemy is to be found within our own ranks,'' Mohn said. ''The enemy you face is at least visible. The insider might be the brother who smiles at you with a dagger behind his back.''

The Japanese man made a slight gesture. ''But is

that not the greater challenge? To unmask the friend who would betray you? To kill a hundred strangers with a bomb is child's play. But to outwit the one who hides in your own shadow and behind the mask of a smile? Such a challenge offers greater intellectual stimulus.''

A slow smile of appreciation creased Mohn's face.

''Murakawa, I feel we are more than just brothers in adversity. Your words remind me of myself.''

''YOU'RE SAYING WE TAKE our orders from you now, Rick?''

Jardine rounded on the speaker, eyeing the broad-shouldered man who sported a near shaven head.

''That going to be a problem, Scott?'' he asked.

''Hell, I guess not,'' Scott replied. ''Just as long as we know.''

''Well, now you do, so let's get to it.''

The Black Dawn terrorists broke up, each moving to his appointed station. Jardine had assigned a select number to patrol the exterior, while the remainder took up guard duty near the entrance to the actual facility. Beyond secure doors was the laboratory complex where the Armageddon Virus was being produced and sealed in small pressurized containers. The production staff was under a lot of stress, with Mohn's orders still ringing in their ears. His demands that they complete their assignment well ahead of the previous target had them working nonstop. They were taking shifts. There was always one group on duty, while the other rested and ate. Mohn, despite the urgency of the situation, had realized that overtired workers were liable to make mistakes, and a mistake with this virus could result in any number of deaths.

Jardine pushed his way through the facility doors and stood in the deepening twilight. He gazed across the compound to the chain-link fence and gates. Beyond were the buildings of the computer software division. They were dark and empty now, the workers having finished for the day. They were already well on their way back to their homes in and around Mason's Crossing.

The area around Sand Bluff was theirs now. They controlled it. No one was going to break in and cause any problems. Not as long as Rick Jardine was in charge.

He turned and dispersed his group. They were all armed with automatic weapons, SMGs and handguns. Each man wore a headset and throat mike so they could stay in contact with one another. No one would get inside the compound without being spotted. And once they were picked up, Black Dawn would deal with them quickly and without mercy.

20

They had abandoned the Cherokee, hiking the final miles to Sand Bluff. Chet Raven knew the land, and he took Bolan in a wide circular route that brought them in behind the towering cliff. The final assault presented them with a long, arduous climb. Their destination was the top of the bluff, overlooking the facility. Needing the isolation, Mohn had built his compound against the base of the bluff.

The climb might have been a near impossibility for anyone unfamiliar with the terrain. Raven seemed to know every rock, every handhold. He skirted areas where loose surfaces might present danger, or create noise that might give them away. Jenny Cade, Bolan quickly realized, was in tune with Raven. She was as much a part of the land as he was. Bolan's respect for the pair grew with each passing hour.

They made the last stretch of the climb as the daylight faded, leaving the rugged landscape bathed in glowing red.

Bolan and Raven carried coiled ropes slung over their shoulders. These had come from the rear of the Cherokee where the deputy kept emergency gear. Raven also had a leather pouch slung from his shoulder. Before moving off, the deputy had taken the 12-gauge Ithaca police special shotgun from its rack, along with a waist belt holding extra shells.

"We'll take a break," Raven said. He led them on a few yards, and as they rounded a weathered outcrop Bolan caught the silvery gleam of water splashing its way downslope.

As the soldier knelt and splashed the cool water on his face, Raven squatted beside him.

"Still find it hard to take in," he said. "I had a feeling Meinster was up to something, but I never had any notion it would be as serious."

Bolan raised his head after taking a drink.

"It's just the way I told you," he said. "They have to be stopped here before they start to distribute the virus. If they get it out to their people, they'll be able to go anywhere they choose. Just walk in and place one of the containers. By the time the activator releases the virus, the deliveryman is long gone."

Cade wrapped her arms around herself. "And they'll do it? Just drop a container and let people die?"

"They're planning a terror campaign," Bolan explained. "They want to inflict enough suffering on the public to raise awareness of their existence. It's a form of blackmail intended to force the government to the conference table so that Black Dawn can be accepted as a legitimate party."

"You can't be serious," Raven said. "The American people aren't going to stand for crap like that. Give political clout to a bunch of murdering terrorists?"

"The neo-Nazi movement has enough of its own believers. They'll give it strength. Black Dawn is only one group. There are other white supremacist organizations who would join such a movement. Chet, these people prey on the weaknesses of others by hammering home stories of ethnic groups taking the bread out of the mouths of true Americans. How they push their way into the country, taking our jobs, our homes. In unsettled times, people can be seduced into a way of thinking that could make Meinster and his policies seem right.''

''Along the lines of Hitler and the Nazi party?'' Cade said.

''Meinster's role model. His father was a loyal Nazi. He brought his son up to believe it was the only way. And Meinster does. If he could swing it, he'd have us all saluting the swastika.''

''You believe he wants to involve this Black Dawn in Germany as well?'' Raven asked.

''If he can produce his virus in quantity, I think he'll supply it to Black Dawn in Europe. They'll go for broke, initiate a massive terror campaign and try to rally enough support to force the issue of political acceptance.''

''What about the Japanese visiting the facility?'' Bolan glanced at the woman.

''I know there are factions in Japan who would jump at the chance to create havoc over there, extreme groups who have similar ideals to Black Dawn. Maybe Meinster is trying to build an alliance with the Pacific Rim and have America boxed in on both east and west seaboards.''

The deputy didn't say anything. He was staring off into the twilight, his expression bleak.

''Bill, we want to help,'' Cade said.

Bolan turned to her. ''You already are. Jenny, I

don't want to put you on the firing line. Once this thing starts it's going to get ugly. Black Dawn isn't some soft-center protest group. They're terrorists plain and simple.''

''I wasn't volunteering to go in with guns blazing,'' she said. ''But there must be something I can do.''

''I need a pair of eyes up here. Once I get into the facility I won't have any idea what's going on outside.''

Bolan pulled a compact transceiver from his backpack and handed it to her.

''I'll be carrying one of these. If you need to contact me, just press the button and I'll hear you.''

The woman took the transceiver. ''You've got it.''

''How far to the top?'' Bolan asked.

Raven stood, pointing.

''We should make it in twenty minutes. If we cut off that way, we're directly over the facility.''

''Let's go,'' the Executioner said.

They moved off, walking the darkening slopes with care. Caution was a constant companion now. Even though Raven and Cade knew the area and tackled it with confidence, it took no more than a step in the wrong direction for them to plunge over some unseen crevasse.

Bolan's mind was working on his target area even as he made his way up the dizzy heights of the bluff. The facility below was an unknown quantity, the layout a mystery. His only advantage lay in surprise. The strike he made would need to be hard and fast, with no time for doubt and less for mercy toward his enemy. Black Dawn had a total disregard for human life. That suited Mack Bolan. The lines had been drawn, and he was more than willing to step over them.

If Black Dawn wanted to deal in the dark world of violence and sudden death, then they were going to find themselves up against a master of the craft.

THE NIGHT SKY LOWERED around them. There was a pale moon and a few stars, but enough light for Bolan to do his work.

The deputy had led them to the spot he said overlooked the facility. Bolan had walked to the edge, peered over and saw that the upper lip of the bluff curved outward, hiding the view of the facility.

"Trust me," Raven said. "It's below us."

"I don't doubt you, Chet," he said. "Just tell me how far below."

Raven smiled suddenly.

"Around 150 feet," he said.

"We got enough rope?"

"You let me take care of that."

Bolan sat and pulled off his backpack. He pulled out his Uzi and a double magazine. Snapping it into place, he placed the weapon on the ground and took out his combat harness. The pouches were already filled with spare magazines for the Uzi as well as for the Beretta and the Desert Eagle. The soldier also carried a half-dozen fragmentation grenades. He peeled off his trousers and shirt, exposing the blacksuit. Raven glanced up from laying out the rope and watched Bolan shrug into the harness, checking his weapons carefully.

"You really mean to do this, huh?"

The soldier nodded.

"I'll go down with you," Raven said, "and provide backup while you go in and do whatever you have to."

Bolan didn't question the deputy's offer, or his motives. The man was a law officer. This was his job.

"Chet, leave me that pistol you took off Erlich," Cade said.

He passed it to her without a word. The young woman checked it and tucked it behind her belt.

"One thing I need you to do," Bolan said to Raven. "When I get inside and you hear the shooting start, you take out any vehicles in the area. And the chopper if it's on the pad. I don't care how you do it, or how much noise you make. I just don't want anything left that can be used for a getaway."

"Consider it done."

"The same goes for anyone who gets by me. Nobody leaves the facility, Raven."

The deputy stared at him for a moment, then nodded.

"We can't afford the chance of someone getting away because they might be carrying samples of the virus or information about how to produce it."

"Never thought of that one," Raven said. "Message understood."

The Executioner slid a gleaming knife into a sheath on his belt.

"Any guards on the outside we deal with as quietly as possible," Bolan explained. "The less warning they get inside the facility the better."

Cade touched Raven's arm, her eyes fixed on his shadowed face.

Bolan sensed her concern and spoke directly to the young deputy.

"Chet, if it's something you can't do, tell me now. I won't ask you to get involved if you feel it's wrong."

Raven breathed deeply. He touched the knife sheathed on the left side of his belt.

"No problem, Bill. I won't let you down. You have my word."

Bolan smiled. "I don't need your word, Chet."

They laid out the rope. Raven selected a point back from the edge of the bluff. He pulled steel pitons from the bag slung from his shoulder. There was a short-handled hammer in the bag, and he used it to drive a couple of the steel rods into the solid rock. Looping the free ends of the ropes through the holes in the pitons, Raven secured them.

"We'll have to go down hand over hand," he said to Bolan. "Take it slow, feet braced against the rock face. The surface is sound, so you won't find it crumbling underfoot. About two-thirds down, there's a natural ledge wide enough to take us both. It's a good chance to rest. We'll come down on the roof of the building. It's flat and butts right up against the rock face. The facility goes into the face. There are natural caverns inside. When the place was originally built, the caverns were used as a means of expanding the work area."

"You have any idea what Meinster has done to it since he took over?" Bolan asked.

"Nothing detailed," Raven said. "We picked up some local talk from the people working in the software building. They were never able to see inside, but they did mention construction crews working in the fenced-off compound. They worked twenty-four hours a day to finish whatever they were doing.''

Bolan slung his Uzi.

''Jenny, no heroics. If any of Meinster's people show up, you stay out of sight if you can. Don't give them any reason to hurt you.''

''I should've brought my frying pan with me,'' Cade said.

Raven grabbed her by the shoulders. ''Damn you, Jenny Cade, listen to the man. I want you alive when I get back from this. Not blown all to hell because you figured you could handle the bad guys by yourself.''

She stared at him, eyes wide at the intensity of his outburst. A word began to form on her lips, but it was lost when she threw her arms around him and kissed him.

''Take your own advice, Deputy.'' She threw a long look at Bolan. ''You make sure he comes back to me, Bill Rawson, or I'll haunt your dreams.''

''Believe her, Bill. She'd do it, too.''

They picked up their ropes, tying loops around their waists and throwing the excess rope over the edge of the bluff. Pulling the ropes taut, they walked backward over the lip, following the curve of the rock face. Raven knew his rock climbing and took the lead, with Bolan following at a steadier pace.

The darkness shrouded them, turning them into phantom figures descending the empty face of the bluff.

A soft, warm wind blew from out of the wasteland. It tugged at their clothes, only gently, but even Bolan sensed that if it grew stronger they might find themselves in difficulty. He concentrated on the descent, ignoring everything else. He closed out the night and listened to the sound of his own breathing and the faint scuffing of Chet Raven's boots as he led the way down the bluff.

The sweep of the overhang slowed them. They had to negotiate the outward curve, then the sudden concave underside of the bulge. Raven passed hushed words of advice that Bolan followed without question. Even so he missed his footing a couple of times and banged against the hard surface of the rock face. Once, for dizzying seconds, he hung suspended from the rope, fingers gripping it tightly as he spun slowly from side to side. Raven called out from below, telling him how to bring himself back under control. Bolan followed the directions, lowering himself hand over hand until his feet met the outward curve of the rock face below the overhang, and he was able to stabilize himself again. Raven called a rest, giving them both time to catch their breath and prepare for the next stage.

It seemed like an interminable descent, walking down the face of the high bluff, with nothing to indicate how far they had come, or how far they had to go.

The minutes built up. Ten. Fifteen. And then twenty by the time they reached the ledge Raven had promised. There they were able to sink to the hard surface and rest with their backs against the bluff, sweat trickling down their faces as they pulled cool air into their lungs. Their muscles screamed from the effort of the descent, protesting against the abnormal loads that had been forced on them. Their fingers ached from gripping the coarse rope.

"They say people do this for enjoyment," Bolan said.

Raven managed a soft chuckle. "And others join the Sheriff's Department so they can have a quiet life."

"How much longer?"

"We'll reach bottom in less than ten minutes," Raven said.

"We going to have enough rope?"

"We might run short," the deputy admitted. "There're plenty of natural hand- and footholds from here on down. If your rope does give out, you'll be able to make it fine."

Bolan stood, ready to move on.

They climbed over the ledge and started down. Raven's prediction about the handholds proved to be correct. The surface of the bluff was ridged with natural humps and hollows, the majority of them offering sound grips. Bolan found he was depending less on his rope now. He was able to negotiate the way by using hands and feet. When he felt his rope start to pull, he loosened the waist loop and freed himself from it. Minutes later he was standing beside Raven on the flat, dusty roof of the building.

This was Bolan's territory. Raven stepped back and allowed the Executioner to take command of the situation. The deputy knew his limitations. He was happy to let Bolan run the show from here on.

21

Rick Jardine had just completed his third check, contacting each of his outside guards over their headsets, and had received satisfactory confirmations from each man. Even so he wasn't completely happy with the situation. Something nagged at him, quietly chewed at his insides. He poured himself another cup of hot, black coffee and sat back in the chair that had previously belonged to Klaus Erlich, his brain constantly churning over the details that were lodged there.

And then he knew what was bugging him. He reached for the telephone and called a couple of his people into his office.

The damned bluff itself! He'd forgotten about that!

When the pair came in, he quickly laid out his instructions.

"Take one of the trucks, get to the top of the bluff and check it out. Stay up there if you figure you need to."

The pair turned to go. One of them paused.

"Rick."

"What?"

"You expecting some kind of trouble?"

"Larry, the way things have been going the last

few days, I'm expecting something. Right now I don't know what. Or from where. Which is why I'm trying to cover all the bases."

"If we run into anybody up there?"

"Take them out. Just get rid of them. If they're dead, they can't do a damn thing. I don't want you hauling in any fucking prisoners. You hear? We don't have time to look after them."

"About damn time," Larry said. "Too many of our people are dead because we been pussyfooting around."

"So make certain we don't lose any more," Jardine said. "Take whatever you need from the armory."

Larry nodded and pushed his partner out the door, leaving Jardine alone again.

He pushed away from the desk and paced the office, his eyes roving over the maps and schematics pinned to the bare walls.

Jardine paused in front of a schematic layout of the facility. He followed the line of the chain-link fence that cut it off from the software production area. The fence was electrically charged with enough power to fry a side of beef. There were cameras on it, relaying images that covered the whole area, and at night the floodlights would have lit up a baseball field.

So why was he still uneasy?

Because he'd known secure installations to be breached before. There was always a weak point, some spot that had been overlooked, ignored because no one had thought it could be used to gain entry into the restricted area.

Some place like the bluff itself.

Jardine stared at the diagram. That had to be the place. It was the only section not covered by cameras or fences, because Erlich had decided in his wisdom that it wasn't going to cause them any problems.

If anyone was going to try for a breakthrough, he was going to use the face of the bluff.

Jardine reached for his phone.

"Carl? Listen, I want another check on the patrols. Complete. No excuses. If there are any breaks, I need to know right away. I'll be with Mohn."

Jardine left his office and made his way to the next level where the German had his office and conference suite. The talks with the Japanese were over. The Crimson Shadow group had retired for its own discussions, leaving Mohn to oversee the ongoing production of the virus.

Checking the office, Jardine found Mohn behind his desk, head down as he studied computer readouts. He glanced up as Jardine gave a perfunctory knock before stepping inside.

"Problems?"

Jardine closed the door.

"Trying to head them off," he said. "I'm expecting visitors. I also have a feeling I know which way they'll come in."

Mohn's eyes gleamed with interest.

"Have you acquired an ability to see into the future, Rick? Have you been consorting with the local Indians and taken up mysticism?"

Jardine ignored the taunts.

"No, but I did figure out what Erlich the wonder boy missed."

"Shame on you, Rick, speaking ill of the dead. So what have you spotted?"

"The fact that he didn't do a damn thing about protecting our backs. The fucking face of the bluff is wide open. Didn't he ever hear about rock climbing for Christ's sake?"

Mohn stood. He opened a desk drawer and lifted out an automatic pistol, checked that it was loaded and ready for use. Opening his jacket, he tucked the weapon behind his belt.

"I've sent a couple of the men to drive up there. The trouble is, it's going to take them some time. Right now I've got Carl making a radio check on all the outside patrols."

Mohn muttered to himself in German, his voice low.

As Jardine turned to go, the telephone on Mohn's desk rang. The Nazi leader snatched it up.

"No, but he is with me. What do you have? Damn! Check again. I don't care. Check again."

Mohn slammed down the phone, his face taut as he tried to control the anger rising in him.

"How many?" Jardine asked.

"Two. Carl is sending one of the others to investigate. I've ordered him to make another sweep."

Jardine pulled open the door.

"I'll get everyone on full alert," he said.

"Let us hope it's not too late," Mohn snapped.

CROSSING THE CONCRETE yard in front of the main entrance to the facility, Lyle Bekhausse checked the Uzi he was carrying for the third time.

Though he wouldn't have admitted it to anyone verbally, he was nervous. It was fine belonging to

Black Dawn, and he believed in everything the movement stood for. But there was no guarantee of immunity from death. Paying your dues didn't offer you invincibility. The fact had been proved positive over the past few days by the deaths of a high number of Black Dawn followers. Bekhausse had known some of the dead. Friends from Chicago. He had been lucky, coming here to New Mexico as part of Mohn's protection squad. It had been considered an honor. Now he wasn't so sure. Klaus Erlich was dead. Not that anyone was going to mourn his passing. The German had been a pain in the ass. Throwing his weight about, constantly belittling everyone around him as if they were dirt under his boots. The man had been a prize idiot, which was being polite.

The important fact was that Erlich—as clever as he figured he was—had died so easily. Which showed them all they were just as vulnerable.

Bekhausse turned the corner of one of the stacks of crates that were piled around the compound. One of the roving guards was supposed to be in this section. He was one of two who hadn't responded to the check.

The area was deserted. Because of the stacked crates there were dark corners and areas that even the floodlights didn't penetrate. The gunner moved along the row of boxes, checking.

He saw a pair of downturned boots poking out from between two crates, and a cold shiver of fear tracked along his spine.

Bekhausse reached for the transmit button on his headset.

As he did, a whisper of sound reached him from behind. He turned, trying to swing his Uzi on-line.

As he spun, he caught a glimpse of a black-clad figure coming at him, silent and very fast.

He saw a flash of something, cold, clean metal, and felt something slash across his throat too quickly for him to understand what was happening. And then there was pain. Blood began to spill down the front of his leather jacket, and he began to choke. The night swelled up before his eyes, shutting out the sound and the sight of the black-clad figure watching him.

Bekhausse was on his knees, then on his face, pressed against the rough concrete. His left hand was spread out against the ground, close to his face, and the last thing he saw was the Black Dawn tattoo on the back of his hand. As the darkness crowded in, Bekhausse could hear a voice in his ears. It was Carl, checking with him through his headset.

Carl was asking if there was a problem.

As MOHN AND JARDINE entered the radio room, Carl Brecht raised a hand, showing three fingers.

"Bekhausse has just gone off the air," he stated.

"Four to go," Jardine said under his breath.

"Get more men outside," Mohn snapped.

The security boss snatched up one of the phones.

The distant sound of an explosion reached his ears. He looked up and saw Mohn staring at him. The expression in the German's eyes wasn't pleasant.

"A thought just occurred to me," the Nazi leader said.

Jardine stood with the receiver in his hand.

"Unless this local policeman, Raven, is some kind of infiltration expert, I have a feeling our friend Belasko has just risen from the dead."

22

Bolan had spent some time checking out the lay of the land, with Raven beside him pointing out what he could recognize. The soldier had identified the electrified fencing and had watched the movement of the cameras set up on the perimeter. Their movement showed that they were set to scan the exterior of the compound, covering only the immediate area inside the fence. As Bolan was already inside, the cameras weren't going to cause them a great deal of worry.

"The main entrance is below us. As far as I recall from the original design, they're just a pair of glass doors. Meinster could have changed that. If he doesn't want anyone inside the place, he might have installed steel doors with a security lock."

"I'd do it if the place was mine."

Raven pointed across the compound.

"The loading ramp at the far side of the building is blocking off the helicopter pad. You still want it taken out?"

The soldier nodded. He motioned Raven to silence, then indicated the figures patrolling the compound below them. He'd counted seven of them during the time he and the deputy had been checking the area. The men were armed. The high-intensity lighting made the compound as bright as day, so Bolan had no difficulty spotting the headsets the guards were wearing.

"Chet, every man down there is equipped with a headset and probably a throat mike. That means they'll have instant contact with the people inside. I'd guess they have someone on-line all the time, able to pick up anything those guys say. That means they'll be able to pass the word pretty fast. It's going to make our job that much harder. We have to take them out as quickly as we can. No time for thinking about it. Remember what I said? Hard and fast."

They stayed on the roof for a while longer, checking and rechecking the movements of the roving guards until they had the routes implanted in their minds.

"I'll take this side of the compound. You cut around so that you can get near the loading ramp. From there you can check out whether the chopper is on-site. If it is, you hit it once the noise starts. If not, just look for any transport and deal with it. Then keep an eye on the gates."

Raven nodded. "No one gets out."

They moved toward the rear of the roof, intending to climb down away from the compound frontage.

The Executioner went first, hand over hand down the last twenty feet of the rock face. The moment his feet touched the ground, Bolan unslung the Uzi and cocked it. He covered Raven as the young deputy made his descent. Staying close to the wall, they moved to the front of the building, ducking beneath windows as they passed by. At the front corner they crouched in the shadows and waited.

Bolan had timed their movements to coincide

with the patrolling guards. His calculations had left them with enough time to reach the ground and gain the front of the building before the first of the returning guards passed the spot.

Placing his Uzi on the ground, Bolan slid his combat knife from its sheath. Despite his acceptance of what had to be done, Raven failed to repress a shudder as he saw the knife. He watched the cold length of sharpened steel in Bolan's hand. The moment the blade appeared, it seemed to mold itself to the Executioner's fist, becoming an extension of his arm. A part of him. Just as silent and deadly as the man himself.

Bolan raised his left hand in a signal. The soft sound of the guard's approaching footsteps reached Raven's ears and he eased back, giving the soldier room to maneuver.

The guard stepped into view, armed with a stubby Uzi. A headset curved across his shaven skull. He wore dark pants and shirt, and polished combat boots. He was checking the area ahead of him, not seeming to be paying any attention to the side of the building where Bolan and Raven were crouched.

When the Executioner moved, it came as a complete surprise to Raven, even though he'd been expecting it.

Bolan rose from his crouch, taking a single, loping stride forward that brought him up behind the guard. The soldier's left hand snaked around the man's neck, his big hand clamping tight over the guy's mouth to cut off any warning yell. Bolan pulled back sharply, yanking the guard's chin up and back, the move exposing the guard's throat. For a moment it lay taut and naked, completely exposed to the cutting sweep of Bolan's combat knife. It was over almost before Raven realized. He only saw the gaping wound for a second, then it was lost in the sudden gush of bright blood. The guard's lean form began to wriggle, as if he were trying to pull himself free, but Bolan held him fast as the wriggling became a series of spasmodic shudders. Moving back into the shadow of the wall, the Executioner lowered the corpse to the ground. He quickly rolled the dead man against the base of the wall, sheathing his knife before he scooped up the Uzi, then turned to Raven.

"You ready?"

The deputy nodded.

Bolan touched him on the shoulder, turned away and was gone around the end of the building.

The moment he moved off, Bolan put Raven out of his mind as he stalked the next guard. The deputy was on his own now. He would stand or fall by his own actions, and there was little Bolan could do. In combat every man was on his own.

Chet Raven was about to face his own baptism of fire. He had been forced to kill once already. This time he would have to take life in a deliberate act. It never became easy.

The thoughts evaporated as Bolan spotted his second guard. The man was talking as he moved, one hand pressed to the headset. He finally broke the connection, both hands back on the Uzi he carried. He was dressed in a similar semiuniform as the first guard. Where the other man had been lean and of medium height, this guard was over six feet, broad and powerfully built. Bolan took note of the physical build as he slung his Uzi over his shoulder, drew his combat knife and crept on silent feet behind the guard until they turned at the end of a stack of empty wooden crates.

It was there that Bolan made his strike. His method was exactly the same as before. One hand closed over the guard's mouth to cut off sound. As the man's head came back, Bolan felt the guy react. The Executioner's muscles were put under pressure as the guard fought back. The gunner's hands let go of the Uzi, and he reached up to snatch at Bolan's.

But the moment he'd closed off the guy's mouth, Bolan struck with the knife, and his deep, slashing cut was faster. The razor edge bit deep as it was drawn from left to right, going in so deep it severed everything it passed over. The guard arched violently, nearly lifting Bolan off his feet. The Executioner was flung from side to side as the dying guard raged against the terrible wound and fought the losing battle to stay alive. His blood pumped out in crimson streams.

Bolan felt the struggles ease. The guard slumped forward, slamming against the stacked crates. He went to his knees, body twitching as the soldier laid him facedown, sliding him between two of the crates.

Turning away, Bolan crossed the open compound. He was counting off the numbers, aware that he had less than a minute to breach the entrance now. The next pair of guards who worked this section of the facility would be there soon.

His way in would have to be forced, as quick as he could make it.

Bolan's immediate plans were changed even as he emerged from behind the stack of crates. He had taken no more than a couple of steps when he saw an armed man moving across the compound, heading in his general direction.

One of the other guards was way off his normal patrol path.

Why? Had the alarm been raised?

Bolan doubted it. If it had, the whole place would have been in uproar by now.

His only assumption was that the two dead guards had failed to call in when they should have, and this guy was coming to check if there was an explanation.

Bolan turned aside, ducking out of sight beside a second row of crates. He waited until the guard had walked by him, then followed. He could hear the guy speaking to someone on his headset.

The guard snapped his submachine gun into position as he rounded the stack of crates ahead of Bolan. He made it so far along, then stopped as he saw the feet of his fellow guard.

The Executioner didn't hesitate. He pulled the knife as he increased his pace, coming up behind the gunner just as the man began to turn. There was no time for finesse this time. Bolan brought the blade around in a savage sweep, the razor edge ripping its way through the man's soft throat and laying it open from ear to ear. The guard fell back, blood pouring from the wound. He dropped to his knees, then fell face forward.

As the soldier backed away, he picked up the faint sound of someone calling the dead guard through the headset.

This time he made a run for the main entrance. The doors were set back beneath a roofed overhang. Bolan had only to take a quick look to confirm that the transparent doors were probably unbreakable glass and could only be opened by the keypad set into the wall beside them.

He took two of the fragmentation grenades and pulled the pins. He let the levers spring and counted off the seconds before lobbing the bombs at the doors and ducking back behind the protection of the outer wall.

The detonations shattered the glass, blowing deadly shards inside the entrance area. Smoke billowed out in a hazy cloud.

The moment the glass had stopped falling Bolan went in, his Uzi up and tracking, and brought Black Dawn's war to its own doorstep.

CHET RAVEN'S PROGRESS across the compound went without challenge. He had memorized the paths the guards took, and he utilized the natural cover provided by stacks of equipment, empty packing cases and metal drums that were scattered around the area. Twice he had to duck for cover as he spotted the roving guards, but luck stayed on his side and he reached the loading ramp safely.

He knew he was going to have to face the enemy sooner or later. In his heart Raven hoped he would be able to do it with his shotgun in his hands and not the cold steel of a knife. If pushed, he would have gone that route. His preference was the distance a gun would allow.

Peering across the ramp, the deputy saw the dark bulk of the helicopter on the landing pad. There were two armed figures close by, scanning the area.

The cop was deciding his next move when Bolan's grenades went off. They alerted him, as well as the two guards. With the echo of the explosions still in his ears, Raven broke from cover and sprinted across the compound. His eyes were on the helicopter, and as he rounded the end of the loading ramp he saw the two armed figures moving out from the aircraft.

One of the gunners pointed in Raven's direction. The second man immediately veered toward the deputy, leveling his Uzi. He cut loose, the first burst chipping the concrete in front of Raven. The deputy swung up the shotgun, jamming the butt to his shoulder, triggering a single shot. His long hours of practice paid off as the concentrated burst took a bloody chunk out of the gunner's right shoulder. The man stumbled, cursing loudly, his own weapon forgotten in his pained confusion. Raven didn't allow him the luxury of recovery time. He fired a second shot, this time taking a moment longer to aim. He saw the gunner go down, his chest blowing open in a burst of red.

As Raven turned to track the other man, he heard the metallic chatter of the gunner's submachine gun. The deputy felt the concrete spit out splinters at his legs. He turned aside, desperate to remove himself from the direct line of fire. The subgun rattled again, and slugs plucked at Raven's clothing. He threw himself down, the air punched from his lungs as he bounced against the pavement. He rolled, twisting his lean body so that he was facing the advancing gunner.

The Black Dawn terrorist skidded to a stop, giving himself a moment to aim the Uzi.

Raven had already pointed the muzzle of the Ithaca at a shallow angle, picking up the terrorist as

the guy drew to a halt. Ignoring the demands of his
air-starved lungs, the deputy touched the trigger.
The scattergun went off with a solid boom, the
charge hitting the gunner over the heart. He cata-
pulted backward, his face registering shock. He hit
the concrete on his back, his skull smacking against
the ground with a solid thump.

The deputy got to his feet and raced to the helicopter. He pulled open the access hatch and reached
inside for the signal flare gun racked next to the
pilot's seat. He broke the action and saw that the
gun was loaded. Backing off, Raven turned the shotgun on the aircraft's fuel tank, racked in a fresh
cartridge and blew a pattern of holes in the cover
panel. Fuel began to spill out, splashing onto the
concrete. The cop fired another round, opening the
tank even further. At a safe distance he cocked the
flare gun and fired it into the middle of the spilled
fuel. It burst into flame, reaching back to engulf the
rear of the helicopter.

Raven had already ducked behind the loading
ramp. He heard the roar of flame as it expanded,
then set off the rest of the tank. It blew with a dull
roar, the resultant fireball illuminating the entire
compound as it rose into the night sky.

23

Smoke and dust swirled around the entrance area, debris falling around Bolan as he breached the shattered doorway.

A gunner lurched around the open doorframe on the far side, one arm raised to ward off flying plaster.

Bolan triggered a short burst of 9 mm fire, cutting the terrorist down before he could ready his own weapon.

Without breaking stride, the soldier crossed the foyer and stepped over the downed man. Ahead of him a long corridor led directly into the heart of the building. A number of doors lined both sides of the corridor, leading into offices with large glass partitions that allowed Bolan to see whether they were occupied.

Ahead of the soldier a door was flung open and two men burst through. Both were armed with Uzis. The lead man opened fire while he was still trying to clear the doorframe, and the spray of slugs shredded the ceiling panels and shattered fluorescent lights, showering Bolan as he pulled hard against the opposite wall. The Executioner lowered the muzzle of his own weapon and fired a return burst. His targets were practically stationary, caught in the narrow confines of the doorway, and the Executioner's blast cut them into bloody shreds. They tumbled back into the office, blood spraying from their torn flesh, faces peppered with splintered glass from where Bolan's volley had caught the wide partition.

Through the glass farther along, Bolan saw other adversaries, alerted by the gunfire, already snatching up their weapons and turning for the doors. A number were white-coated technicians. Others were clad in the semiuniforms Bolan had seen on the guards outside.

He leveled the Uzi and fired through the glass, blowing it out of the frames and into the rooms. The moving hardmen were caught in the glittering shower, faces and hands slashed by the deadly shards. Switching his aim, Bolan repeated the action, his bullets mingling with the broken glass, leaving men yelling and running for cover.

Plucking grenades from his harness, the Executioner pulled the pins and hurled the projectiles through the empty frames, dropping to the floor a moment ahead of the twin blasts. The explosions reverberated through the building, the air suddenly full of shattered debris. Dust and smoke clogging the air in the corridor.

Bolan regained his feet and moved ahead, his submachine gun emitting short bursts as he met token resistance from the dazed and injured defenders. There was no forgiveness in the Executioner. He faced his enemies, and he dispensed justice with brutal efficiency.

A badly wounded guard lurched along the corridor ahead of Bolan. The left side of his body was slick with dark blood. He slumped against the wall, one hand reaching to open a heavy metal door. He sprang the catch and pulled the door open, falling inside even as Bolan fired at him. The 9 mm bullets raked the wall, clanging noisily against the steel door. The soldier paused to reload the Uzi, then slung it over his shoulder. He pulled out the Beretta, setting the selector switch on 3-round-burst mode.

The wounded Nazi suddenly appeared in the open doorway. He was carrying an M-16, and he opened fire, filling the corridor with 5.56 mm slugs. His fire was indiscriminate, the shots gouging the walls and ceiling, taking out more glass.

Bolan dropped to the floor, raised himself on one arm and sighted in with the Beretta. His first burst caught the Black Dawn terrorist in the upper chest. The following three rounds cored his skull, spinning him back against the doorframe. He bounced forward and crashed to the floor.

The Executioner pushed to his feet. He stepped over the dead guard and found himself staring into a small-arms store. Racks of weapons lined the walls, mainly M-16s, but some Uzis and Ingrams as well. There was also a shelf supporting a neat line of LAW rockets. The selection reminded Bolan of the arms caches he'd seen in and around Chicago. He reached inside and grabbed three of the LAWs, slinging them. He picked up a double magazine for the Uzi and snapped it into place.

Back outside, he moved along the smoke-filled corridor. At the far end he was faced by a flight of stairs that led off to the right. These would take him to the upper floor. Directly ahead of him was a solid door that bore the sign Software Packing Department. Bolan had the feeling there was something far more lethal on the other side.

The Executioner raised a booted foot and kicked the door open.

As it crashed back against the inside wall, Bolan went through, his Uzi up and tracking as he sought his targets.

AUTOMATIC FIRE CONTINUED behind Chet Raven. He felt the shocking impact of a slug as it dug into his left arm. The force of the bullet spun him, and in a blur the deputy saw an armed figure coming at him. He tried to lift the shotgun, but it was in his left hand and had suddenly become too heavy. His fingers loosened, and the weapon slipped free.

The armed man grinned as he saw Raven's shotgun drop.

"This is where you get your ass shot off, Indian," he said, unable to resist the remark.

Raven knew he was as close to death as he was ever going to be. His life could be measured in seconds, so whatever he did had to be right the first time. And he had to do something. If he let himself be blasted by this grinning, bald moron, Jenny would never forgive him.

Nor would she ever let Rawson off the hook, and he wouldn't wish that on his worst enemy.

Raven's thoughts were flashing through his head in the same instant the Black Dawn terrorist was mouthing his words.

Suddenly, dropping to the ground, he rolled, taking himself away from the Nazi's line of fire. It brought the guy back to the real world, and he reacted by jerking his weapon around, triggering wildly. His action sent a stream of slugs into the concrete, following Raven's rolling form.

The deputy felt something burn through the soft flesh of his right calf. It was like being stabbed with a hot poker. The pain made him yell, but it also spurred him into action. His right hand clawed for the butt of his holstered Beretta 92-F. Pulling it free, he thumbed off the safety and as he came to rest on his back he pushed out his right arm, the autopistol lining up on the gunner.

The trigger pull was never smoother. Raven felt the weapon push against his palm as he kept on triggering, the Beretta spitting out a stream of 9 mm Parabellum bullets that chewed at the gunner's chest and throat. The guy let out a strangled scream as his vocal cords were reduced to bloody pulp. He fell over sideways, blood spurting from his ravaged throat, and crashed to the ground, his wiry frame bending like a bow. The fingers of one hand tried to claw up the concrete before he went slack and died.

Chet Raven, bloody and bruised, but still alive, fought the desire to lie down and rest. He staggered to his feet and retrieved his shotgun. He also picked up the dead terrorist's Uzi. The deputy located a couple of spare magazines and tucked them in his belt before turning and limping his way to cover behind the loading ramp. He slumped to the concrete behind a pile of metal boxes.

Before he did anything else he made sure that all his weapons were fully loaded and armed. The next time they came looking for him he was going to be ready.

And if he got out of this alive, he knew he'd never complain about life being dull and boring again.

THE 4x4 PULLED ITSELF over the final rim of the slope. Ahead the top of Sand Bluff lay empty and silent in the moonlight. The truck coasted across the bumpy surface, then came to a stop.

The Black Dawn terrorist named Larry stepped out, armed with an Uzi and an automatic pistol.

He waved for his partner to step out.

"Sounds like Rick had the right idea," Larry said.

Both men could hear the crackle of gunfire coming from below the bluff.

"Right maybe," the other man said, "but too damn late."

Larry snapped the cocking bolt back.

"Let's check the place out. If we find anybody up here, they're dead."

The pair moved away from the 4x4, separating as they advanced across the bluff. Larry cut off toward the edge that overlooked the facility. His partner circled, coming in from farther along.

It was Larry who spotted the pitons hammered into the rock and the two ropes snaking out of sight over the edge.

"Hey, I found something," he called. "Looks like this is how they got down."

Kris ran across to join him, and they stared at the ropes.

"Way too fucking late," Kris repeated.

The sound of the truck engine bursting into life alerted the pair.

"Goddamn it!" Larry yelled.

He turned and saw the 4x4 roll forward, picking

up speed as it headed for them. The headlights came on, blinding the pair. Larry dug in his heels and moved away from the bouncing vehicle. He stumbled and went down, burning his hands on the rock as he hit the ground.

Kris wasn't as lucky. He hesitated too long. The left front fender caught him, and he was thrown across the bluff before vanishing over the edge, his fading scream lost in the roar of the truck as it curved around, away from the overhang.

Larry yanked his Uzi around, triggering at the dark outline of the truck. He heard the metallic clangs as slugs bounced off the steel body. Glass shattered. One of the side windows blew out. Larry pushed to his feet, trying to settle his aim on the hunched figure behind the wheel. He fired as the truck hit a dip in the rock, the stream of 9 mm bullets burning a line across the hood.

The 4x4 braked, coming to a dead stop, its engine stalling.

Larry ran toward it, circling around. He cleared the front and saw that the driver's door was open. He fired off a burst that punched into the compartment, then realized that the seat was empty. He looked around and saw a slim shape moving away from the rear of the truck. Larry followed.

"You fucking piece of..."

He moved around the rear of the 4x4, the Uzi up, searching the way ahead. He wished he was back where he belonged. His home ground was Chicago. The city. Not this dusty, sun-bleached chunk of nothing.

Larry stopped and peered around.

Nothing. No sound. No movement.

Then he picked up a soft rustle behind him, so soft it was almost nothing. Except that Larry knew better. Somebody was behind him.

His suspicion was confirmed when he heard the metallic click of a hammer cocking back.

Well, go to hell, he thought, and spun on his heel, the Uzi firing as he held the trigger back.

The burst from the machine pistol was followed by a dull impact that took him between the eyes. Larry didn't even have time to react as the 9 mm slug burrowed into his skull, blowing out the back of his head in a dark spray. He completed his turn and fell facedown on the hard rock of Sand Bluff, his blood spidering across the pale stone.

Jenny Cade stood in the two-handed firing stance for a long time, the pistol pointing at the empty space. She let out a long, trembling breath as her reaction set in, and she sank to the rock before her legs gave way under her.

The woman sat staring into the darkness, the sound of the distant gunfire rising from the facility below. She was only just realizing what she'd done. But up to that point her only motivation had been the knowledge that somewhere not too far away, Chet Raven was involved in something dangerous along with Bill Rawson. They had both put themselves in the firing line, exposing themselves to whatever Black Dawn had secreted inside the Sand Bluff facility, and there had been no way she could have simply sat back and not done something to help.

THE LARGE OPEN WORKSHOP spreading out in front of Bolan was filled with a combination of computer terminals and laboratory equipment. The long benches and cabinets, the white-coated technicians and their armed minders, told him he was in Mohn's production area.

His sweeping glance showed him the restricted area at the far end. Here, behind sealed glass walls, was the section that was the heart of the facility, the secure lab where the Armageddon Virus was being manufactured.

Bolan's sudden appearance wasn't entirely unexpected. The exchange of gunfire and the grenade detonations had forewarned the Black Dawn operatives inside the workshop. The Executioner's presence drew exactly the reaction he had been anticipating, which was the reason he went through the door with his Uzi up and ready.

As he crashed through the door, confronted by an armed guard on the raised landing above the workshop, Bolan struck the first blow that was to mark the beginning of the end for Black Dawn.

The Nazi terrorist lunged at the Executioner, his automatic pistol leveled to blast the intruder. Bolan kept moving forward, the opposite of what the guard had anticipated. The soldier's right forearm swept up and smashed against the guy's face. The blow spun him sideways, a cheekbone cracking under the force. Bolan followed up by jamming the muzzle of his Uzi into the guard's side and triggering a short burst that shattered the man's ribs into splinters. The terrorist was knocked off his feet, tumbling down the flight of concrete steps to the floor of the workshop.

Bolan dropped to a crouch, freeing one of his grenades. He sprang the lever and tossed the high-explosive into the middle of the room, then flattened himself against the rough wall. The detonation shook the whole building.

Yells and screams filled the air.

Gunfire, directed at Bolan, added its noisy clamor. Bullets scored the wall over the soldier's head, striking the stone pillar that protected him. He stayed down, picking up the rush of booted feet closing in on his position. He waited until the advancing guards were almost on him before turning his Uzi loose, spraying them at almost point-blank range as they reached the top of the steps. His relentless stream of fire cut down the front faction of Nazi terrorists, tumbling them down the steps, sending the others scattering for cover.

Bolan removed the spent magazine and slammed in the second one during the brief lull. Crouched against the base of the pillar, he heard movement in the corridor behind him. The soldier reached for the Desert Eagle, pulling it clear of the holster, and, half rising, he turned.

He picked up the armed figure leaning around the doorframe. The guy was still searching for his target when Bolan triggered the massive handgun. The .44-caliber hollowpoint slug took away the side of the guy's skull, spinning him back along the corridor in a mist of blood.

Grabbing the edge of the door, Bolan slammed it shut, then turned to face the workshop again.

Firing the big handgun four more times, the single shots took out armed guards as they tried to rush him. Then he reholstered the weapon and took up the Uzi again.

The survivors of his initial attack had retreated to

the far end of the room. They were clustered against the sealed glass partition, behind which Mohn's people were working on the virus itself. The work had come to a standstill. The personnel behind the glass, clad in biohazard suits and breathing piped air, were staring out through the panel, wondering what was going on. Some of them were banging on the thick, soundproof glass.

Bolan had checked out the workshop. This was part of the natural cavern that went into the bluff itself. The roof of the large room had been hung with fluorescent lights, and the walls were festooned with electric power cables and pipes carrying water. The only access to the room was the door Bolan had entered, which placed him in a double-edged position.

The enemy couldn't get out except through Bolan.

And he was caught between two forces, one on each side of the door.

The Black Dawn terrorists on the other side of the door worried Bolan less than the ones inside the workshop. His attention was drawn to the sealed area. Even at the distance he was from the lab, he could see the complex array of equipment, the mass of tubes and receptacles being used in the production of Mohn's virus.

Bolan had come to Sand Bluff to destroy the Nazi leader's capability to produce the Armageddon Virus. His secondary task was to eliminate the Black Dawn followers who were willing to go along with the Nazi's deadly scheme.

There was no hesitation in Bolan's actions as he slid two of the LAW launchers from his shoulder. He extended the tubes, arming the weapons. With the first on his right shoulder, he leaned out from behind the pillar and sighted the room. He triggered the charge and the missile leaped toward the workshop, over the heads of the Black Dawn terrorists.

Bolan didn't wait to see the result of his handiwork. He simply tossed aside the smoking tube and picked up the second. He repeated the action of the first, sending the rocket toward the sealed lab.

The first projectile struck, shattering the sealed glass as it detonated. The explosion was followed by a second as the next missile struck. The blast spread out, filling the far end of the workshop with flame and smoke. An echoing crash rose above the blast as gas bottles blew, adding to the destruction. Flames raced to the ceiling, sweeping overhead and bursting the fluorescent tubes.

Unslinging the Uzi, Bolan raked the surviving Black Dawn guards as they rushed the stairs, his scything blast shredding flesh and dropping the terrorists in their tracks.

He spun as the door behind reverberated to a heavy thud. The Executioner was in time to see the door swing open, revealing a group of armed men crowding forward. He triggered the submachine gun, firing into the bodies, and saw them fall back.

One guard avoided the volley, ducking through the door to confront Bolan face-to-face. He swung the Uzi he was carrying, catching the Executioner across the side of the head. Bolan rolled with the blow, then kicked out with his booted foot, knocking the guy in the chest. The Nazi slammed into the wall. He arched his body, pushing back at Bolan, swinging the Uzi again within the close confines of the landing. The soldier ducked and slammed his fist hard into the man's exposed groin, which drew a strangled grunt. Without pause Bolan followed through, delivering a savage fist that connected with the guard's lower jaw, snapping his head back. Blood sprayed from the guy's slack mouth. A forearm smash twisted the guard's head around. Bolan caught hold of his hair and slammed him face-first into the stone wall. The Nazi sagged to the floor.

An odd roaring sound reached Bolan's ears. He threw a glance over his shoulder and saw a gathering mass of curling flame engulfing the far end of the workshop. It started to sweep toward the ceiling, gathering speed as it sucked greedily at the air, then was suddenly, frighteningly, racing across the ceiling. The boiling mass of fire was seeking any source of air coming into the cavernous room.

The open door where Bolan was standing.

The Executioner turned and took long strides, throwing himself through the open doorway. He hit the floor on one shoulder, rolling frantically to the side, burrowing his face deep in the protective circle of his arms as the thick tongue of flame exploded through the door and along the corridor. He felt the heat sear across his exposed back, and his lungs drew in the superheated air.

Bolan's brain told him to move, to get away from the inferno before it devoured the very air he was breathing. He recalled the staircase, knowing it had to be close by. Raising his head, he located the stairs. He was lying alongside the bottom step. The soldier gathered his legs under him and lunged up off the floor, reaching for the wall to pull himself up the risers. The heat followed him. His lungs were burning from the lack of oxygen. There was no second chance if he didn't make it. Bolan drove himself up the stairs with the stubborn instinct for survival that had pulled him out of difficult situations on more than one occasion. The flight seemed endless, and the fire was snapping at his heels. Tears stung his eyes. His body wanted to stop, to rest. He forced out the reserves of strength that propelled him up the stairs and onto a square landing. But a fire door denied him access to the corridor beyond. He slammed his shoulder against it, yet the solid door refused to budge.

Smoke was curling up the stairwell, starting to thicken.

Bolan retreated back down the stairs, his fingers dragging the final LAW rocket from his shoulder. He fumbled the catches that would enable him to extend the tube and prime the launcher.

Kneeling on a step, the LAW resting on his shoulder, the soldier blinked his stinging eyes. The door above him seemed a thousand miles away. He aimed the launcher, his finger stroking the trigger. He had no time for finesse. No second chances.

He snapped the trigger fully back, felt the LAW pulse as it discharged its missile. Dropping the tube, Bolan buried his head into the protection of his arms.

The rocket impacted against the door and destroyed it. It also took out a section of the supporting wall, the blast exploding into the corridor beyond, sending debris flying.

Bolan pulled his Uzi into position, ejecting the used magazine and replacing it. He pushed to his feet, cocking the weapon as he drove to the top of the stairs.

Stepping through the smoking ruins of the doorway, Bolan breached the second level of Kurt Mohn's Black Dawn lair.

24

Mohn attempted to pacify the Japanese delegation. Only Murakawa responded, even though he was concerned.

Osugi expressed his thoughts loudly and with little regard to any form of protocol.

"This is what we get for listening to you— old man. Coming here has involved us in this fool's problems. His promises are nothing. He can't even protect his own people."

Mohn was unable to understand Osugi's rapid Japanese, but he didn't need a translation. The tone of the young man's words was enough to make him realize that his alliance with Crimson Shadow was on shaky ground.

He pushed that to the back of his mind. Protecting his base and the virus was his priority. Until that was secure, then the rest could go to hell.

He turned for the doorway as more gunfire followed the grenade blasts. He pulled open the door and motioned to the armed man in the corridor.

"Find Jardine for me. Now!"

As the guard hurried off, Mohn caught Murakawa's troubled gaze.

"I'll deal with this," he said and left.

Murakawa faced his group. "Wisdom would dictate that we leave. Our presence in America is far from being legal. If we are caught, things won't go well for us."

The other three Crimson Shadow delegates nodded their agreement.

Murakawa noticed that the fourth member of his group—Osugi—was missing. He heard movement behind him and turned. Osugi was at the door. Tucked under his left arm was the black case that held four of the virus containers, samples of the completed product Mohn had been showing them. In Osugi's right hand was a large black automatic pistol.

"What is the meaning of this?" Murakawa demanded.

Osugi smiled, gesturing with the pistol.

"Get to the other side of the room," he said. "Now."

The Japanese obeyed. All except Murakawa. He held Osugi's gaze.

"You knew this day would come," the younger man said.

"I would've expected more from even you, Osugi."

"Then you are a bigger fool than I imagined."

The old man moved toward him and Osugi fired. The slug ripped into Murakawa's left knee, shattering the bone. The Japanese man slumped to the floor.

Osugi glanced at his watch, stepping quickly backward.

"I've left you a parting gift," he said, a slight smile edging his thin mouth. And then he was gone, pulling the door shut.

Murakawa, despite the pain of his wound, realized what Osugi had meant immediately. He dragged himself around and gripped the edge of the conference table, peering over it.

In the center of the polished table stood one of the virus containers, slender, shining, deadly.

There was a soft click, followed by the hiss of compressed vapor as the container expelled its contents into the room.

MOHN MET JARDINE as he reached the front of the building. He took the Uzi Jardine offered him.

"What's happening?"

"I'm on my way to find out," the security boss offered lamely, trying to maintain his control over a rapidly escalating disaster.

The German pushed past him, heading for the front stairs that would take him to the main entrance.

He was halfway down, with the increasing thunder of gunfire reaching him from below, followed by the detonations of more grenades—this time inside the building.

The Nazi leader was deciding whether to carry on when a bright flash of light caught his eye. He turned to stare out of the window he was passing just in time to see the parked helicopter erupt into a ball of fire. Thick tendrils of smoke curled into the night sky.

The German stared at the rising flame, his thoughts suddenly going back to the Amazon—another time, another life—when all this had happened before. Could one man be so plagued by misfortune? How could this happen when...

A figure appeared at the top of the stairs.

It was Osugi.

The young Japanese man was clutching a pistol in his right hand. Under his arm was the black case containing the Armageddon Virus samples.

The look in Osugi's eyes told the Nazi what was happening.

The younger man brought up the Uzi.

"No!" the Nazi screamed.

Osugi fired without even breaking his stride. The bullet caught Mohn in the side, cracking his ribs and spinning him back down the stairs. The Uzi slipped from his fingers as he sprawled in a bloody heap, not even aware of Osugi stepping over him as he made for the shattered main doors.

It was the powerful explosions caused by the LAW rockets that penetrated Mohn's fogged senses. He raised his head, groaning at the pain in his side. His submachine gun lay nearby, and he closed his hand over it, pushing upright. He slumped against the wall, using it as a prop and began to climb the stairs again.

He had reached the top when the third rocket detonated, this time above him. Blood was sticky against Mohn's flesh, soaking down the leg of his trouser and every breath was an agony. He reached the head of the stairs. The corridor seemed to stretch away for miles. Thick smoke filled the far end.

He stumbled forward, the submachine gun clamped against his side.

The door to the conference room burst open and Jardine appeared.

"They're all dead," he said. "Murakawa, the others. The virus got them."

Mohn waved him aside. "Osugi. He took the samples."

Jardine saw the blood on his superior's clothing. "Are you…" he began.

"Behind you!" Mohn yelled.

He had seen the black-clad figure emerging from the smoke, carrying an Uzi. The man was tall, black-haired, with eyes that pierced into Mohn's very soul.

The German knew he was facing Belasko, the man who had done so much damage to his organization.

Jardine turned toward Bolan and caught the first volley from the Uzi up close. The 9 mm projectiles sheered his torso, spilling blood and organs in a moment of horror.

Mohn locked on to the menacing figure in black, his blood-slicked fingers fumbling with the Uzi's smooth surface. He knew a split second before that his adversary would fire first.

The submachine gun in Bolan's steady grip emptied its magazine into the German's body, climbing from pelvis to chest, the slugs slamming him back against the wall, pinning him there until the weapon exhausted itself. The sodden form slid to the floor, bloody and torn, but still alive. The defiance still gleamed in his eyes as he moved toward his Uzi, fanatical to the end. Right up to the moment when the Executioner triggered two .44-caliber Magnum rounds from the Desert Eagle and shut him down for good.

EPILOGUE

The facility swarmed with federal agents and police. Air ambulances were ferrying the wounded out, and the survivors were already in custody.

Smoke still rose into the clear New Mexico air from the smoldering wreckage of Mohn's virus lab. The area had been given the all-clear after the CDC teams, wearing contamination suits, had gone inside and checked it out. The explosions Bolan had set off had caused a chain reaction as they had interacted with the chemicals and gases being used in the production cycle. The subsequent fire had destroyed the existing virus samples, rendering them harmless. Very little remained of the production area. Bolan's blitz had not only burned the virus, it had reduced the computers and the formulations to ashes.

The Executioner sat in the rear of a 4x4 belonging to one of the teams Brognola had called in. He was drinking a mug of hot black coffee as he surveyed the activity.

He watched the big Fed break out of the ranks of official bodies and cross over to the vehicle.

"I can always depend on you keeping your word, Striker," he said.

"We agreed they had to go down," Bolan reminded him.

"I'm not complaining," Brognola said. "The CDC is mad because you managed to fry every damn virus in the place. There's nothing left for them to investigate. But that's nothing compared to the military. They're griping about being frozen out. They wanted the chance to catch one of the bugs and rebuild it."

"Why do you think I made certain the virus was destroyed in there, Hal?"

"Hell, I know that. They don't. All they see is a lost opportunity to get their hands on a new weapon."

"Don't we have enough to handle without the U.S.A. having the Armageddon Virus locked away somewhere?"

"Hey, time out, Striker. I'm on your side, remember."

One of the FBI agents approached. "All the suspects have been rounded up now, sir," the agent reported to Brognola. "They're ready for transportation."

The big Fed nodded. "Get them out of here." As the agent turned to go Brognola said, "You won't lose any of them over the mountains will you, Brennan?"

The earnest young agent looked surprised.

"Of course not, Mr. Brognola," he said stiffly.

The big Fed watched him go.

"Pity about that," he commented softly.

"How's Raven?" Bolan asked.

"Out of surgery apparently. The doc said he'll make it. He's young enough to pull through. He was lucky. An inch to the right and that bullet in the back would have severed his spine." Brognola smiled. "Anyhow, he didn't have permission to die. That girl of his actually told him so. Made all the difference."

"Glad to hear he's okay."

Facing the Executioner Brognola asked, "One question, Striker. What happened with Raven?"

"One of the Japanese men tried to break out with a sample of the virus, shot Raven in the back and tried to take a car. He didn't make it. Raven had promised me no one would get out alive. He kept that promise."

"What about the virus?" Brognola inquired.

Bolan indicated the burned-out shell of the helicopter.

"I dumped the containers in there while it was still burning. As far as I know, they were the last samples."

Brognola raised his eyes to the clearing sky.

"Striker, I hope to God you're right."

"So do I," Bolan answered.

Killers' ransom...

DON PENDLETON's

MACK BOLAN®

HELLFIRE STRIKE

In an effort to stem the flow of heroin into the U.S., the President issues an ultimatum to the Southeast Asian drug lords. To add some muscle to this diplomatic move, Bolan is sent to deliver a clear message—comply or be eliminated.

The drug lords still have one ace up their sleeve—a tie to the highest levels of the U.S. government....

Available in August 1999 at your favorite retail outlet.

Take 2 explosive books plus a mystery bonus FREE

An old enemy poses a new threat....

JAMES AXLER
DEATHLANDS®
Gaia's Demise

Ryan Cawdor's old nemesis, Dr. Silas Jamaisvous, is behind a deadly new weapon that uses electromagnetic pulses to control the weather and the gateways, and even disrupts human thinking processes.

As these waves doom psi-sensitive Krysty, Ryan challenges Jamaisvous to a daring showdown for America's survival....

Book 2 in the Baronies Trilogy, three books that chronicle the strange attempts to unify the East Coast baronies—a bid for power in the midst of anarchy....

Shadow THE EXECUTIONER®
as he battles evil for 352 pages of heart-stopping action!

SuperBolan®

#61452	DAY OF THE VULTURE	$5.50 U.S. ☐
		$6.50 CAN. ☐
#61453	FLAMES OF WRATH	$5.50 U.S. ☐
		$6.50 CAN. ☐
#61454	HIGH AGGRESSION	$5.50 U.S. ☐
		$6.50 CAN. ☐
#61455	CODE OF BUSHIDO	$5.50 U.S. ☐
		$6.50 CAN. ☐
#61456	TERROR SPIN	$5.50 U.S. ☐
		$6.50 CAN. ☐

(limited quantities available on certain titles)

TOTAL AMOUNT	$
POSTAGE & HANDLING	$
($1.00 for one book, 50¢ for each additional)	
APPLICABLE TAXES*	$ _____
TOTAL PAYABLE	$ _____
(check or money order—please do not send cash)	

To order, complete this form and send it, along with a check or money order for the total above, payable to Gold Eagle Books, to: **In the U.S.:** 3010 Walden Avenue, P.O. Box 9077, Buffalo, NY 14269-9077; **In Canada:** P.O. Box 636, Fort Erie, Ontario, L2A 5X3.

Name: _____

Address: _____ City: _____

State/Prov.: _____ Zip/Postal Code: _____

*New York residents remit applicable sales taxes.
 Canadian residents remit applicable GST and provincial taxes.

GOLD EAGLE®

GSBBACK1